The Fatal Shadow

In the rural peace of the Scottish Highlands, Miss Sophia McLinn, daughter of an
Edinburgh surgeon, stretches her slender
means by running a summer guest-house. But
the night she took in Aline Hillis and her baby
in the depths of winter, she took in trouble.
The trouble was represented by the young
American from the oil rigs whom Aline had
walked out on, and by the local lad for whom
she had deserted him, found shot and drowned
in the loch soon afterwards.

The police suspect the American. Miss
McLinn, surprisingly, believes in his
innocence. But she is preoccupied by the ultra-
cautious advances of a widowed civil servant,
and though she views this staid, careful
suitor with unsparing eye, he is unwittingly
instrumental in exposing her to a viciously
calculated attempt on her life.

When she reveals her attacker's identity to
the police, they are sceptical, but now events
(and Miss McLinn) take over as the story moves
swiftly to an ironic close.

As a narrator, Miss McLinn is unforgettable.
The reader will be beguiled and ultimately
gripped by her account of life in a closed
community out of season as she drily tells
all—or almost all.

GAVIN BLACK

The Fatal Shadow

COLLINS, 8 GRAFTON STREET, LONDON W1

William Collins Sons & Co. Ltd
London · Glasgow · Sydney · Auckland
Toronto · Johannesburg

First published 1983
© Gavin Black, 1983

British Library Cataloguing in Publication Data

Black, Gavin
The Fatal Shadow. — (Crime Club).
I. Title
823′.914[F]   PR6073.Y65
ISBN 0 00 231368 5

Photoset in Compugraphic Baskerville
Printed in Great Britain by
William Collins Sons & Co. Ltd

Our acts our angels are, or good or ill,
Our fatal shadows that walk by us still.
Beaumont and Fletcher

CHAPTER 1

If it hadn't been for the baby I would never have let the girl into the house. That plus the fact that it was winter. There was something else, too, I can only call it a feeling that the situation was absurd, and this made me curious. There she stood, with a drift of late February snow behind her; not a heavy fall at all, light dry flakes whose arrival on us was really accidental, a cloud unloading in the wrong place. It wasn't a cold night, no wind, spring promised, the first snowdrops out along the drive.

I had put on the outer light before opening the door and this sent a strong glow right down over the gravel. The girl's figure was somehow an intrusion into that brightness, the area of her shadow increased by the wide brim of a dark felt hat. It was the kind of hat you might see on a model at a dress show, but never on a street, flamboyant and silly, though this one seemed to have weathered into a certain rigid effectiveness as an umbrella. She was standing well back from the front steps, as though after ringing the bell she'd had second thoughts, on the point of turning away when I opened the door on its chain, as I always do after dark. These days even in Loch Riddoch we have to do that now, open our doors on chains on dark winter nights. Twenty years ago we never locked a door, front or back. Even ten years ago.

The baby seemed well enough wrapped up, first in an embroidered fringed shawl and under that woollies, these grubby-looking even in electric light. There was a de-cided suggestion of grubbiness about the girl herself, drab grey skirt almost touching the ground at the back, a man's brown tweed jacket and a muffler that looked as though she had knitted it, loosely, and hadn't known where to stop. It was twisted twice around her neck and still went down behind the baby, both ends of it, almost to hem level. She carried the child crooked in one arm to leave a hand free. Behind her, on the gravel, was a thing I can just remember my grandmother using, a Gladstone bag. This was big, the soft leather bulging. She also had a raffia-work carrier slung from one shoulder.

I couldn't really see her face, just a chin and the end of a smallish nose, no hint of eyes. I hate not being able to see people's eyes. The dark glasses craze these days usually means that the wearers haven't the courage to look straight at the world and be looked back at. Unscreen their eyes and we would see what nothings they are.

I didn't much care for the girl's voice. It was quiet enough, almost too quiet, a hint of arrogance in this, as though she had never had to shout to get what she wanted.

'Miss McLinn?'

'Yes,' I said.

'You take lodgers.'

It was a statement, not a question.

'Who told you that?'

'Willie the Shop.'

You don't call Willie Menzies 'the Shop' unless you've been in Loch Riddoch for some time, yet I was sure I had never seen this girl about in the village. That word 'lodgers' had come straight from Willie, used deliberately. He enjoys sending me bed and breakfast casuals he knows I will turn away.

'I can pay, if that's worrying you?' the girl said.

I cleared my throat.

'Nothing is worrying me. I have no room for you.'

'Only for a couple of days?'

'No.'

'Just tonight?'

'No!'

I stepped back and shut the door. I switched off the

outer light and turned into a hall lit only by a three-quarters life-size draped male figure holding aloft a lamp, with tinted glass panels, which Daddy used to call our cigar store Indian. He had been twice in America at medical congresses. I think if Ming had still been with me I would have left things at that, going back to my sitting-room in time for the ten o'clock news on the radio. There is something about a Chow which makes a house feel occupied, perhaps it's the bulk of all that fur. Occupied and protected. He did make the house feel like that, particularly on winter nights, when time is the problem, that feeling that it is passing and you're not making any sense of it, sense or use.

But I didn't have Ming to lead me back to the fire. I took only a couple of steps before turning about, switching on the outer light again, and opening the door, this time not on its chain. The girl was only a third of the way down the drive, near where the trees begin, going slowly, bent slightly to one side by the Gladstone bag. It was still snowing but the gravel swallowed every flake where it landed. As though refusing to acknowledge the light reaching past her, the girl didn't turn. I called:

'Wait!'

She stopped walking but didn't put down the bag.

'Have you anywhere to go?'

She didn't answer.

'Do you know where the police station is?'

She started walking again.

What I felt was near-anger. I still don't know why I ran after her. I remember my feet noisy. It must have been the falling snow silencing everything else, making that stilled background for the crunch of my shoes. I certainly hadn't meant to run. When I got to the girl I was puffing.

'It's nearly ten at night,' I said. 'You can't be walking around in the dark with your baby. Where did you come from?'

Her answer was so long in coming she might have been considering whether I was entitled to it.

'The chalets.'

'You mean the hotel chalets?'

'Where else?'

'You were living in one of them?'

'That's right.'

'Then why leave?'

'The man I was with put me out.'

One of those. We see too many of them in the summer, though not usually dressed like this girl. Or carrying babies. The hotel chalets cater for skiers in winter, but in a season without much snow most of them had stayed empty. There was talk of the hotel laying off staff on account of poor bookings for the summer. My own bookings were terrible. I would wake in the night knowing that I ought to put a bed and breakfast sign at the gates but I knew what that would mean; an invitation to Willie the shop which he would accept with relish, sending me all the hand-picked riff-raff who came his way.

The girl had put down her bag. She seemed completely incurious about why I had come running after her. I might have been the supplicant. I resented that. Then the baby started to cry, a snivelling sound, almost the kind of noise a kitten thrown away in a garbage can might make, as though still fighting for life, but without real hope. Suddenly I seemed to hear myself using words that hadn't come from my mind.

'You can stay. Just for the night.'

If she was grateful it didn't show. I let her carry the bag as well as the baby. She was used to it. We walked side by side, the crunching on the gravel all from my shoes, the girl wearing what looked like soft-soled moccasins.

During the summer when I have guests staying I have flashes of sensing how my house must feel to people coming into it for the first time, and I had one of these again. The hall was colder than outside. Even in the warmer weather there is a chill that seems to cling. When Mother was alive we had an electric night storage heater on at low, but even that didn't get rid of the clammy feel. There was another of these heaters in her bedroom, both disconnected now because I can't afford to run them. All I have is the kitchen boiler on twice a week for hot water and a coal fire in the back sitting-room I try not to light until evening. When my lawyer was out seeing me last time he said that since 'Morvern' was my main capital asset I ought to give it proper heating to ward off dry rot. All very well for him making these pronouncements with the fees he charges and his wife with a new Peugeot for herself every second year. Not to mention their centrally heated house kept at seventy. He had the nerve to stand in my drive here looking at my twelve-year-old Austin while telling me that I'd find it paid to trade in at least every three years. I wonder what he thinks I make as an income out of my guests? I've never told him. It can come as a startling surprise when he is sorting out my affairs after I'm dead. That is, if I don't live longer than he does. He looks pretty soft to me, physically.

There wasn't much of a fire in the back sitting-room. I had meant to take a hot-water bottle to bed after the news. I go to bed earlier these nights. Not having Ming has something to do with it. Last thing he always had to be let out, and he went the rounds of our acre and a half checking on everything, his duty to see that all was in order before he went to his basket. Some nights I would hear him barking at something beyond our little wood, probably a rabbit. He caught them sometimes, moving really fast for a Chow, but he always let them go again, and any I saw seemed unhurt. He was a soft-mouthed dog. Maybe soft-hearted.

At the door to the small sitting-room the girl shivered. I wasn't looking at her, but it was something I felt, as though convulsive enough to disturb the air around us. I went over to the fire and whacked at the one lump of coal but there was no glow. I rebuilt the fire from paper, sticks and coal kept in a bucket under the radio table, struck a match, and got up from my knees feeling the sudden burst of heat that really was a waste of money.

The girl had left the Gladstone bag in the hall near the staircase, but had gone on holding the baby in the crook of one arm, her face still shaded from the glare of a central light by the brim of that hat. I couldn't see her eyes taking in the room where I live in winter, but could guess what she was thinking. When my mother could still come downstairs she insisted on big things in this little place, including her roll-top desk which I still use. I have always meant to re-design the room but earlier this year, when I was almost down to doing it, I suddenly had the feeling that any changes made would disturb Ming, and me too, in some way. So I did nothing. And now the girl was standing to stare at what was almost a junk-shop shambles. This irritated me. My voice was sharp when I said:

'Do you have to go on wearing that hat? Or are you changing your mind about staying?'

She took the hat off to drop it on the table, all in one rather slow movement that seemed to involve only her free arm and not the rest of her body. I suppose some would have called her pretty, she was certainly small-featured, very pale with the kind of near-white, almost translucent skin that was once a sure sign of tuberculosis. Ash blonde hair, rather thin, that could have done with a good shampoo and rinse, hung down to her shoulders, as straight as string. I found out later that her pale blue eyes could go even paler, almost as though she was able to drop a screen over them, like movable cataracts.

'Why don't you put the baby down?' I asked.

She did that slowly as she was to come to do everything

she was obliged to in my house, not so much settling the child comfortably in a chair as propping it up there, leaving it to arrange itself. I felt I should have asked the baby's name, but didn't. I didn't find out the girl's until some time later. It was Aline, which seemed to me to sit on her beautifully, as though her mother had been instinctively guided to it all those years ago.

'Would you like a cup of tea?'

She nodded, coming with me to the kitchen. I certainly wouldn't have left a child the way she left hers, in a position from which it could easily have rolled off on to the floor, but that was none of my business so I didn't say anything.

'I haven't got the range on today,' I said. 'It's a relic from the times when we had servants. Or at least my parents did. The thing eats fuel.'

She had no comment on my small talk, just stood there unwinding her scarf, a process which took quite some time, the knitted object then laid on my well-scrubbed table. After that she just stood, no attempt to help me with cups or setting out milk and sugar. I filled the kettle and put it on the fast burner of the bottle-gas cooker. Then I took what was a plunge of sorts.

'Won't this man you were with be worried about where you've got to?'

'No.'

'You're saying he won't care?'

'That's right.'

Perhaps I should have felt pity. Instead I looked at that face which seemed to be waiting to have something with meaning painted on to it. I wanted to shout at her, to ask what she could expect to get out of a life she wouldn't treat with any respect. What I said was calm enough.

'Is the man you were with the father of your baby?'

'No.'

'You haven't been married?'

'It wasn't holy.'

I had no idea then what she meant and it was something of a shock when I found out later.

'Would you like anything to eat? Bread and butter?'

'Yes.'

'What about the baby?'

'He's all right. I breast-feed him.'

I knew now he was a boy. The child seemed a bit old for breast-feeding, but it might be one of the new things. I had read somewhere that in the Far East it can go on for years.

Aline then made a decision without being prompted to it. She pulled out a chair and sat by the table, quite close in to that repulsive piece of knitting, almost as though she was guarding it. While I moved about she inspected my kitchen from this new position.

Every winter since my mother died I have been meaning to paint it white but in spite of good intentions it stays as I remember it from childhood when this was only our summer home, a sort of grease colour. Everything is painted wood, peeling where it has been scrubbed too often, and there are cracks I can never really clean even by poking a knife down into them. The floor is stone with linoleum laid over it, and in winter you could be stepping on an ice floe, even the twice weekly lit range never thaws that floor. Sometimes I find myself staring for a long time at one of those magazine ads offering to install a really glossy kitchen for the positively give-away price of three thousand pounds which I just don't happen to have.

I buttered two slices of the atrocious baker's sliced bread I bring back from our nearest big town, Taybridge. The bread has one virtue; it keeps quite well if you store it in a cool pantry. This is something I *do* have, probably the coolest pantry in the country, with marble slabs giving it the feel of the arctic even on a summer's day. In winter a short visit makes the temperature in the rest of the house seem bearable.

The girl was hungry. It's a fair walk from the hotel chalets to my house even without a baby and a bag. She put away a couple of slices in two minutes, not exactly cramming her mouth, but still chewing steadily. When I asked if she would like more she said she would and I gave her another two slices. She ate them both, along with almost all the butter I would use in three days. I often make do with margarine, and the cooking kind at that.

While Aline was still eating I put on the kettle again to fill hot-water bottles for two beds. I have the old porcelain kind, 'pigs' they used to be called, and I'm told are quite valuable as curios these days. I'm not selling mine; 'pigs' in the beds have become something of a house feature with my summer guests. It was while I was filling one that I decided to put the girl into Mother's old room.

This is over the kitchen, and big, originally meant for three servants, the second warmest place in a cold house, which is why my mother requisitioned it when she moved to Loch Riddoch from an Edinburgh she was sure Hitler meant to bomb. The room had been empty since her funeral, badly needing doing up, paintwork and paper in a terrible state from cigarette smoke, a habit Mother picked up in India while Daddy was still an Army surgeon. She claimed that it was the pre-monsoon heat which had started her off, you had to do something then or you would go mad. So she had taken to forty a day. Latterly the price of these had really bitten into our household budget, but Mother said we could make economies somewhere else, leaving her little pleasures alone. This also meant her sherry, two bottles a week of the best medium dry South African.

I could have asked Aline to help me make up the bed in the room above, especially since I had the feeling that I'd be lucky to see any of her money, but all I did was suggest that it might be a good idea if she attended to her baby.

What I got for that was a look that the Armed Services would have classified as dumb insolence, and no movement from the girl. I left her, going up the back stairs to a musty-smelling apartment in which a bare mattress told me at once that the fitted nylon I normally use for guests would never stretch on that broad bed. This meant I would have to use Irish linen, which was irritating. Then I remembered the servants' sheets, patched cotton, still on the top shelf of the airing cupboard.

By the time I came downstairs again Aline had moved to the small sitting-room and was sitting in a straight-backed chair breast-feeding her baby. It was silly to find this startling, nothing to what you see on television, but somehow in that room it was a shock, almost as though Mother's ghost had risen from what used to be her winged armchair by the radio, shrieking a protest audible only to my ears.

I went over to the roll-top desk and fiddled about in it, as though looking for something. It was ridiculous to go on avoiding looking at the girl, so after a few moments I did look at her, to be at once reminded of Italy, all those Madonnas and child. I must have stared at hundreds of them when I was down there in nineteen-fifty-two, none of them admittedly actually feeding their infants but all of them holding these almost exactly as Aline was doing, as though they were stage props handed to the sitter only a moment before the actual painting began. Neither the girl nor the paintings sent out a strong feeling of mother love.

'You haven't told me your baby's name,' I said with a briskness that was somehow beyond my control.

Aline looked up. She had been staring at a fire needing more coal which it wasn't going to get.

'Pete.'

'He was christened Peter?'

I think she meant to smile, but if so it was an intention rather than an achievement.

'He wasn't christened. I registered him Pete.'

After that I retreated to the kitchen, almost a refugee in my own house, washing up the tea things at a cold tap, and while I was still doing this she came into the kitchen with the baby, wanting to know where her room was. I took her up the back stairs, expecting something of a shock reaction to what was being offered, but though she stood inspecting everything, taking her time over that, nothing was said. I had the thought that this girl's occupancy of the room could be the final phase in exorcising my mother's already fading ghost. All those half-hauntings had been from this base, its memorial silence soon to be violated by a baby's yells.

Not that so far the infant had shown any signs of a noisy temperament. He seemed very quiet indeed, though not placid from stupidity, alert, his eyes always on the move. When his mother had put him on the bed, scrumpling the quilt to give him back support, he sat there with deep blue eyes, almost violet in colour, doing what seemed to be a careful inventory of his new surroundings. I had the odd feeling that there was something almost defensive in this, as though very early indeed he had learned that new environments offered potential threats.

We left the baby while I showed the girl where the bathroom was, explaining that there was no hot water available since I had had neither the kitchen range nor the electric immersion on that day, but there was an electric kettle under the basin which she could use from a plug out in the hall. My guests complain sometimes about no second bathroom, just the downstairs cloakroom, but I have done nothing about that, and I don't intend to. They are paying me less than half of the bed and breakfast charge up at the modernized Loch Riddoch hotel which now boasts private facilities, as they are called, with every bedroom, and asks at least three times my price for an evening meal.

We went down the front stairs, the girl to collect her somewhat scattered possessions, hat in the back sitting-room, scarf in the kitchen, and bag in the front hall. I left her to it, carefully raking out ash from the fire to spare any surviving coal for the re-setting in the morning. Back in the kitchen I listened for any sounds of movement in the room above, but there were none, so I went to lock the back door. Less than three months ago I would have been opening that door to let Ming out, the dog going past me with a courteous flip of his curled over tail. In Taybridge, when I had refused the dog meat that had always been kept for me, the butcher said that the thing to do when you lost a pet was to get another right away, but somehow I couldn't feel that Ming would have liked the idea of that at all. And also I had never thought of him as a pet.

I was turning from checking that the front door was locked when I saw that the girl had left her raffia-work shoulder-bag propped up against the foot of the cigar store Indian. As I lifted it I could see that it seemed to be packed with mostly baby things that she might need, so I took it up with me and went along the passage to Mother's old room, pausing just outside the door to listen, as I always used to do when my parent was alive.

There was a reason for this. Mother claimed that she had never had a good night's sleep since the shock of my brother's death in North Africa during World War II and she also claimed that she had never snored in her life. I used to stand outside her door listening to the snores before I made a diplomatic noise loud enough to wake her and to give her the few seconds she needed to arrange herself against the pillows as the martyr to insomnia who never complains, just bears her cross in silence.

The girl wasn't making any sound at all, though there

was a strip of light showing under the door. I turned the knob.

'I thought you'd want . . .'

I stopped. The girl had pulled up the quilt and had it ballooned out around her as she half sat, half leaned against the edge of the bed. One bare arm was thrust straight out in front of her, the palm uppermost. In her other hand was a syringe, held between fingers, its needle dug into the extended forearm. She was pressing down the plunger with a thumb. A corner of the quilt that had been up like a cowl fell away, taking the shadows from her face. She stared at me, pale blue eyes wide. She shouted:

'Why didn't you knock? Why the bloody hell didn't you knock?'

CHAPTER 2

It was a shock to be screamed at by a total stranger in my own house. In spite of the hour I might have ordered her to get out if it hadn't been for the baby, quiet and invisible somewhere in that huge bed. I said nothing, just pulled the door shut, then went along the passage to my own room. I undressed in the dark, as though hiding from something. When I got into my bed the sheets were icy, I had forgotten my own 'pig'.

I lay there shivering. It was the cold, not nerves. I am not a nervous person. No one who was could possibly have lived all through many winters in a large, empty house which has a wood, and a field, and a stream between it and the start of the village. Ming hadn't been my insurance against being frightened, I had known that I could live alone like this and even quite enjoy it. The truth is that I have preferred living alone in 'Morvern' during the winter to living in it with Mother and her continual complaints about draughts and feeling frozen. On nights when it is windy I do sometimes get a little uneasy, for then the house seems to fill with sounds that can't be explained away, but that doesn't come anywhere near being frightened.

What I had just seen brought me to a kind of fear. It was almost as though, from out of a night offering that pretence of snow, all that is most frightening in our time, the savage wildness of it, had gained entrance into a house whose stone walls had always been a solid defence.

I know nothing about drugs beyond what you read in the papers and a horror of something like heroin addiction may be something peculiar to my generation. The young, with their experimenting, certainly don't seem to feel this. I get the impression from some of them that they have nothing but contempt for the ways in which we deal with stress and depression. One of the few young guests I have had made me quite angry by talk about my generation's action formulas which were really nothing more than bustle for the sake of bustle.

I dare say there is something in this. I hold gloom at bay by keeping busy. Even in the winter there are endless things to be done about this place. It is almost as though the moment my visitors have gone at the end of September I have to start thinking about them arriving again in the spring; for some years I have had a batch at Easter. I do all the redecorating myself, and in a house with fourteen rooms, including four attics, I never want for a job waiting. I like to think, also, that I don't neglect my mind. I rent television for my guests but the set is taken away back to Taybridge the first week in October, which leaves me to get on with my reading. I loathe knitting and crochet and my sewing is mainly confined to patching. I have never made a dress in my life and don't intend to, I would rather wear twenty-year-olds.

We have a travelling library van that would come to my door if I wanted it, but I prefer getting my books in Taybridge, bringing back a dozen at a time on extra tickets allowed me by the girl there as a 'Hardship case', whatever that means. I suppose it could mean the not so young spinster living alone. I believe we are classified as a social problem, though if one of those chits given absurd jobs at taxpayers' expense to go around poking their noses into other peoples' affairs ever came to *my* door she wouldn't repeat the experiment. From what I see, they would be better employed looking after their own generation.

My bed had just started to warm up when I heard the whimpering. It came from some way down the hall, only just human, a wailing pitched above any normal voice level. If I hadn't been certain it was the girl I think I would have been frightened. As it was, I lay perfectly still, even when I made out my name.

'Miss McLinn? Miss McLinn?'

Then she collided with the big blue and white Chinese vase which is just down from my door, capping the wailing with a word I heard first at boarding-school, then daily during my years in the Women's Services, though I can't remember ever having used it myself, even under provocation. These days I may be getting prudish but I didn't care for the sound of it in 'Morvern'.

I put on the bedside light, got up, found my dressing-gown and slippers and, properly dressed for whatever was to come, went across the floor to the door to the hall. Those near sheep bleatings had stopped. I switched on the powerful central light and the glow from this reached firmly to the stair banisters when I opened the door. There was no sign of the girl. I had to go out into the hall to locate her.

If that wailing had been to awaken my interest she had now abandoned the attempt to do this. She was standing by the double window which looks over the drive, staring down, leaning forward as far as she could, but kept from actually getting up to the glass by a shelf of potted plants. While I watched she brought her arms up from her sides and folded them across her breasts, seeming to hug herself, as though cold. She had left the tweed jacket in the bedroom and I saw that the trailing grey skirt was part of a dress with elbow length sleeves. Light behind her didn't make her turn.

There was another light, reflected off plate glass, flaring as though a torch had been pointed up at the house, then cut off.

'No!' the girl said to herself.

'What is it?'

She didn't turn at the sound of my voice.

'Don't let him in, please!'

'Let *who* in?'

'Dean.'

'Is that the man you've been living with?'

'Yes.'

The front doorbell rang.

'How do you know it's him?'

'I saw his face. When he shone the torch up.'

The bell rang again. I put on the light in the upper hall. The girl had braided her hair in two pigtails, the ends secured by rubber bands. I got the feeling it was something she would do on going to bed whatever state she might be in at the time, the ritual automatic, a tradition from childhood still clung to. Hair pulled back like that ought to have given her an air of innocence, but as she turned to face me I didn't see that. I was looking at an actress playing a role for which she had been miscast.

'I've decided I don't want you in my house,' I said. 'If he has come to take you back that will suit me.'

I switched on the light in the torch held aloft by the cigar store Indian and started down the stairs. The bell rang for the third time, now with the man's finger held on it, squandering my battery. The girl leaned over the railing that runs along part of the upper hall.

'Miss McLinn, please! Please let me stay! I can't . . .'

I stopped and looked up.

'Can't what?'

'Go back to him. I'll explain if you'll just not let him in. Don't open that door, please!'

'I am *not* having a drug addict under my roof. Even for one night!'

'You don't understand! I swear I'm not!'

After what I had seen that was nonsense. I went on down the stairs, pretty certain that the girl wouldn't follow. The man outside must have seen a glow from the fanlight, for he had stopped ringing. I put on the outside light.

The chain on the door is stout. A man came specially from Taybridge to fit it when we began to have trouble in the village from louts attracted by the new pool parlour annexe to the Loch Riddoch hotel. If things go on the way they are I dare say we will soon be needing peepholes in our doors. The latest development is respectably dressed men calling at houses pretending to be antique-dealers looking for stock but actually, according to the police, on reconnaissance for burglars.

I opened the door to the limit of its chain. The man spotlighted out there was wearing jeans, a woollen check shirt open at the neck, this mostly red, with a furlined unzipped anorak over that. He had no hat and his very fair, almost white hair looked as though he had been pushing fingers through it. Behind him was that windless, padded silence so strange with us, where the air is almost always stirring. An occasional snowflake still came drifting gently into the area of light.

'What do you want at this time of night?'

My tone was probably harsher than I meant it to be. It

certainly provoked him into an apology.

'Look, I'm sorry. It's just that I have to see Aline, that's all. Speak to her, I mean. I know she's here.'

It was an American voice. During the war I had some practice in placing from their accents where in that country their soldiers came from. This man was Southern. Even when agitated he didn't push his words out in a hurry.

'You could have phoned,' I said.

'Aline, just don't answer phone calls, ma'am. Half the time.'

'She says you put her out.'

'Strictly not true. I only said git when she said she was going anyway. To a guy in this village. Maybe you know his name. Murdo Menzies. You see him around plenty.'

That was true enough, you do.

'What do you mean . . . going to him?' I asked.

'Set up with him, ma'am. Just that. So I'm plenty mad. I let her walk straight past me carrying that bag and the kid and everything. I could have got up to open the chalet door for her, but I didn't. She had to put down the bag to do it.'

He still wasn't talking fast, but the words came as though he had pulled out a stopper and couldn't get it back in again.

'So I just sat there, ma'am. I just sat there. It seemed for hours. I didn't see it was snowing until I got up and went out on the porch. Let me see her, ma'am.'

'She says no.'

He didn't seem to notice that I had spoken.

'I could have come after her in the car. But somehow I had to walk. Maybe I thought that this guy Murdo and she would hear a car coming. I dunno.'

'Have you been drinking?'

'A couple of shots, that's all. This guy Murdo's not in the village. Away in Glasgow or somewhere. I had to wake his old man in the shop. He didn't like that much. He didn't know when the hell his son would be back. Excuse me, ma'am.'

The apology seemed to be for having said hell.

'If you had come in your car,' I said, 'I would have been only too pleased to have you take the girl away from my house. But you seem to have forgotten the baby.'

'No. I just want to talk to Aline, that's all.'

'You can talk to her in the morning. Come back then.'

'Tomorrow I got to catch a 'copter back to the rig. I work on one of the damn things. Out in the North Sea.'

I still wasn't having a scene in my house, particularly not at this hour.

'Come back as early as you like tomorrow. You can talk to her in your car then. I'll see that she goes out to you. Now I'm shutting this door. Don't try to put your foot in it.'

'I won't,' he said.

With the door shut I stood still for a moment, certain that he was doing the same on the other side of the panels. I put out the light above him. As I made for the stairs his face stayed sharply in my mind, a boy's face for all the six feet and more of him, as if the conversion to man hadn't quite come about yet. I had an impression of something else, too, beyond his looks, not so much of innocence, the young these days never seem to me to look innocent, but perhaps the next thing to that, of inexperience which had suddenly been subjected to a great deal of experience and had been swamped by it. His eyes had held an appeal for help much more effective than anything he said.

The upper hall was empty. The girl had put out the light there and in my bedroom, as though she had wanted to listen from semi-darkness. I followed her down a passage with two turns in it. This time I did knock on her door, twice. There was no answer. My mother had been more afraid of help not reaching her if she needed it than of burglars and there had never been a key in the lock. I turned the handle expecting darkness in the room beyond, but there was light of a kind, the bedside reading lamp on its adjustable arm pulled out over the bed and so far down that about all it did was put a bright white spot on a crumple of bedding. In a reflected glow from this I could just make out the girl sitting propped against pillows, a pigtail down over each shoulder. I was reminded of Mother sitting up like that pretending a total disinterest in the food I was bringing, though it would be empty dishes that I later carried down to the kitchen.

'I sent him away,' I said.

'Thanks.'

'He'll be back in the morning for a talk.'

She didn't say anything. In that tumble of quilt, blankets and sheet I couldn't see any sign of the baby.

'Where do you keep that stuff?' I asked.

'What?'

I repeated the question. My own voice surprises me sometimes, it can hit a harsh note. It began to do this when I was commissioned in the war and had to be in charge of my squad on square drill. It was up to you to make the girls jump to it, and I did.

This girl was still against pillows.

'Your drugs!' I said. 'Heroin, I expect?'

I heard the intake of breath. She shook her head.

'I don't really do it! I never have? It's only sometimes. Like tonight.'

'What I saw looked practised.'

'No! I'm not! I mean, I haven't. Not for months. It's just that what had happened made me. I needed it. Don't you see? It's like that. Only now and then.'

It was the longest speech I'd had from her. I didn't believe a word of it.

'Are you going to tell me where you keep it? Or am I

going to have to search this room?'

She sat straight up in the bed then, but her protest was feeble.

'What's it to you?'

'I'll tell you,' I said. 'I'm not having anyone taking drugs under my roof. Understand?'

She understood all right. I didn't have any trouble getting what I was after. I put on the centre light and then went straight for the Gladstone bag. She was a throw-everything-in packer but on top of the mess was a square wooden box with an elastic band around it and a bright label on the lid: 'El Vino Cigars, Best Cuban Leaf'. I pulled off the band. A quick look was enough. I had no curiosity about what was inside. I put the band back on and went to the door carrying the box, the girl's eyes certainly on my back, probably watching me with hatred.

Sometimes, while the rest of the Highlands are still held by winter, we get a private preview of spring in Glen Riddoch, the loch bright blue suddenly, the whole valley cupping surprising warmth, and our mountain, Ben Tala, spends these mornings shredding what clouds are left, letting them stream away from its summit like torn pennants.

The reprieves never last long. Usually by afternoon the overcast is back, with rain or sleet, but the rationed miracle of a glittering morning usually manages to pull me out of the house, most often to walk the road along the shore which leads away from the village towards a forest of huge Scots pines which goes on for miles along the south side of the loch. Ming used to be with me, celebrating too soon an end of winter, barking for no reason, looking back at me as he did it, making sure of an audience.

The morning after Aline's arrival in my house was bright enough, but it wasn't the glitter which got me up, it was my bedside alarm, and I rose feeling underslept and weary, which is not the way I face most days even when I have my summer guests. I dressed, and went down to the kitchen to have a cup of tea after putting a match to the range which was all set and ready. On the way out I picked up the stick I usually take with me to the village these days as a defence against Murdo Menzies's mongrel, a half Collie, half Alsatian with a vicious temper and a rumoured reputation as a sheep worrier. Chows are not prone to fighting, but when they do make an enemy it is for life and Murdo's mongrel was Ming's. I don't even know the brute's name, but since my loss of Ming it has turned his attentions to me, and if I have no stick with which to threaten a wallop he comes sneaking out of a lane, belly down and growling, threatening my ankles.

Twice I have complained to our policeman about these attacks, but there has never been actual evidence of a bite. Even if there had been, Hamish McWilliam, our constable, is within nine months of his pension, his time between then and now dedicated to doing even less than he always has. The Queen's peace could be said to be kept in Loch Riddoch on the principle that if no action is taken on anything that happens the unpleasantness will in due course blow over. The constable knows what I think of him, for I have made that plain enough on more than one occasion.

I wouldn't lay any claims to being one of the more popular residents of Loch Riddoch village. Actually, 'Morvern' really isn't really part of the village at all, flowing between me and it is the river Tala which drains the loch. Crossing what becomes little more than a stream in summer is a narrow, stone, humped-back bridge of the type which General Wade built all over the country when it was his job to suppress the Scots. There is absolutely no evidence that our bridge is genuine Wade, much more likely it is only about a hundred years old and a rather

indifferent copy. There have been three collisions on this
bridge in my time here, these occurring for the very
simple reason that, owing to the hump, you simply
cannot see what is coming at you from the other side.
Very sensibly, the District Council engineers proposed
to replace this bridge, which was becoming unsafe and
would be expensive to repair, with a modern one of
reinforced concrete. The howl of protest which went up
against this was quite astonishing. Our Minister, whose
church I do not attend, is reputed to have called on the
Lord to defend us from those who would vandalize our
heritage, which of course included me since I was all for
the project.

There was much more than that. At a meeting of our
local Preservation Society one of the rose-growing retired
ladies, of whom we have a fine selection, all housed in
new bungalows of singular architectural hideousness,
accused me of being one of the kind of English incomers
who are blighting our Highland way of life. Since I
haven't a drop of English blood from either my father's or
my mother's families I rather took exception to this and
made use of the correspondence columns of our local
paper to say so, which was probably foolish of me. The
net result of this is that there are certain sections of the
community who still feel, four years later, that I don't
rate a nod when met in the village street and we still have
our old humped bridge in spite of a near fatal accident
right in the middle of it just last summer.

I was still on the 'Morvern' side of our bogus antiquity,
but already keeping a lookout for Murdo's mongrel,
when, from a distance, I heard the first loud sound made
by man that morning, a car coming fast from the
direction of the hotel and its chalets. By the time I was
over the bridge the car was at the crossroads ahead, and it
didn't carry on along the main road to Taybridge, but
turned towards me. From the way the driver changed

gears on the corner he didn't have much respect for his vehicle.

It turned out to be a small yellow Fiat driven by the American called Dean. He braked when he saw me, then got out of the car.

'You're much too early,' I said. 'No sounds of her being up and about when I left the house. I came out to meet you.'

'Yeh?'

He seemed much more confident this morning, almost a note of belligerence in his manner. Behind him was the village, no smoke coming from any of the chimneys and no one stirring along the street. There wouldn't be, either, until the Sunday papers arrived, these only reaching us about the time the church bells are making their pretty hopeless bid to challenge the London tabloids.

'What did you want to see me about?'

No 'ma'am' for me this morning. He had surprisingly dark eyebrows to go with that pale hair, not black, but certainly brown, and under them eyes that were nearer green than blue. I held out the house key.

'That's for my front door. And it is not for you to go in and have a talk with the girl. It's for you to go in and get her out of there, with her baby and her bag. To take her back to the hotel chalet.'

'No!'

'She's your responsibility. I don't want her in my house.'

'You took her in.'

The belligerence was still there. It irritated me.

'Listen! I'm giving you a chance to get the girl out of there quietly. If you can't do it, or she won't leave, I'll have to get the police to evict her. The mobile police from Taybridge. I'm simply not having a heroin addict in my house.'

'She's not an addict! Well, not all the way.'

'What would you call her? A half addict?'

He took a deep breath. I could almost hear his lungs crackle in the process.

'Ma'am, please keep her. Just till I get back. A couple of weeks.'

'Absolutely no.'

'Look, like I told you, I got to get to the rig today. I'm out there for two weeks. So I can't do anything about this. I mean I can't hang around. Not for the time it would take to get Aline back the chalet. God, I know how long she takes over things. I got to go, you understand? I miss that 'copter and I probably miss my job. I already got time off to go to my Dad's funeral back in the States. That's where I've been. For three weeks. I had to stay looking after Mom and Sis. That's when this Murdo thing blew up, I guess. Though maybe it was going on before.'

'What Murdo thing?'

'He's going to fix her up in a store. A kind of boutique. Selling tourist junk.'

'Here in Loch Riddoch?'

'Yup. He only wants her for a lay. Sorry, ma'am.'

He had gone soft on me again.

'Stop apologizing,' I said.

'Okay. Sometimes I wish to hell I could hate her. Really hate her.'

'Maybe you haven't been trying hard enough,' I suggested.

'I've tried. I can't do it . . . let her go. It's not *here* for me to do that.'

He was prodding his chest with a forefinger in what had to be the approximate area of his heart. It was absurd and pathetic at the same time, this huge young man standing at the side of a Scottish Highland road on a bright morning, pointing to his heart. He looked totally alien, as though the place in which he now was had nothing to do with him, and never could have, something he had been put down in by accident, no choice involved at all. But there must have been choice in it; presumably he had brought the girl here, she wouldn't have brought him, not a girl with that English voice bringing a man into the wilds. Before she came up here her idea of the country would be the banks of the Thames a few miles up beyond Reading. It wasn't remarkable guessing that he had deposited her in that chalet to be well away from any drug source during his spell out on his oil rig. But the cure hadn't worked, and, from what I had heard about goings-on up in those hotel chalets, there had never been a chance that it might.

The young man reached into a pocket in his jeans to remove what had been a bump lying on one hip. It turned out to be a roll of notes. He held them out to me.

'I don't know what you charge, ma'am. But this ought to be enough, I guess. At least until I get back. I'm kind of short just now. On account of being in the States. I mean in cash. I got plenty in the bank. I could give you a cheque . . . ?'

'I'm not taking your money and I'm not keeping your girl,' I said.

He stood looking at me for what must have been half a minute without speaking, and when he did speak it was just one word:

'Please.'

He didn't spoil that by any bid to suggest that what he was asking was a reasonable proposition, just waited another half minute before saying 'Please' again.

I shook my head. He dropped the roll of banknotes on the grass verge of the road and while I was still shouting at him not to be a fool had got in the Fiat and started the engine. I bent to pick up the notes, meaning to shove them at him through the open driver's window, but he was in reverse and away before I had even straightened, driving on the mirror, revving the engine. He didn't try to turn the car until he was fifty yards down the road and already in the village. All I could do was stand there with his money in my hand while the Fiat swung around our war memorial and took the road to Taybridge, the noise of its engine seeming to wake the morning.

I waited until I was in 'Morvern's' drive, sheltered by my own trees, before I counted the money. There was three hundred and twenty pounds. I was sure the boy had not only emptied his wallet but his pockets as well.

I didn't go in the house, turning away from the front door when I already had the key in my hand, to walk in the garden. Spring growth would soon be threatening after the months of peace from this. In Mother's time, or at least until near the end of it, we had an old man from the village two days a week, and after that I tried doing without anyone at all, but with my guests in the summer this became absolutely impossible and I had to have McKindrick back again. He came, surly as always, muttering to himself while he worked, and charging twice what he used to. The upgraded hotel and its chalets have upgraded our labour costs in the area by at least a hundred per cent in the last few years to a point where even the rose-growing ladies have started to complain bitterly about what they have to pay for a cleaning woman.

McKindrick doesn't now have much to do beyond weeding the gravel drive and cutting grass with the old motor-mower Father bought for his country estate of five acres. I got rid of all the flowerbeds and with no blooms to brighten up its granite frontage the house looks even more gaunt than it used to, the bare windows, from which I stripped yellowing lace curtains after Mother died, give it almost a naked look. Still, my guests seem to feel that the view of Ben Tala and the loch is worth the long trip to get here from England, where most of them come from. On fine days I put deck chairs out on the grass, even giving them tea there when they want it. Old-fashioned smiling service is what I aim for even if I don't always achieve it, and I have to admit that sometimes, while waiting on patent fools, I find myself curdling inside.

The curdling has become worse in the last year or so. In common with probably ninety-eight per cent of the world's adult population I have a recurring fantasy about what I would do if I suddenly won a vast sum in one of those lotteries for which I never buy a ticket. It is rather a coarse fantasy, I'm afraid, I see myself coming into the dining-room at 'Morvern' as though nothing out of the ordinary had happened, wearing my best boarding-house-keeper's smile and carrying a tray laden with steaming food for my hungry guests. I would then just drop the tray in the middle of the worn Turkey carpet, offering the assembled company the highly unladylike two words once used to me by my platoon sergeant when I caught her behind the PT centre under a soldier, these simply: 'Bugger off!' I could have had the girl court-martialled, but I didn't. You might say I took her point. Probably Mother was right: the Services did coarsen me almost to the point of rubbing out my nursery training plus an expensive private education at St Lucinda's High School for Girls in Edinburgh.

I walked on what my father used to call our lawns, but which are now just grass, still clutching the American boy's money in one hand, and thinking about him. There was no point in wondering just how he had got himself tied in with Aline, emotional accidents as bad, and even worse than this, happen every day. I had been the victim of one myself, long ago certainly, but you remember. And with a kind of pity for both the parties involved, though in this case I couldn't muster much for Aline. None at all, in fact.

I had reached the back courtyard when I heard the crying. It was coming from a slightly opened window in Mother's old room: the baby, not a loud sound, not aggressive, undemanding even as a complaint.

I stood still. It was the crying of the unwanted. I might even have sounded almost like that myself once, though not as a baby, alone after John had told me that he was pushing on from our affair to another. When he was killed less than two months later in a dogfight over Occupied France I found myself with a question about the other girl, whether she was as torn as I was. There was never any answer. I never saw her, though she became a face in my mind.

Aline's baby didn't sound as if he expected to be heard, or noticed if he was, though in time the girl would probably get around to baring her breast, or change him. You made a noise in the hope of being attended to eventually. Suddenly there was no need for a decision about whether or not to allow the girl to stay in my house. This had been made for me. I put the boy's money in the pocket of my car coat.

CHAPTER 3

My father used to say that no true Scot would ever begin a new day without porridge for breakfast, but then he wasn't running a boarding-house, and ever since I started with paying guests it has been corn flakes or stewed fruit, and in winter I don't have the fruit, just the packaged stuff, then toast and tea. I had finished with all three when the kitchen door opened and Aline stood staring in, the dark passage behind filling in the frame around her. She was barefoot, wearing only a long pale pink nightgown of what looked like flannel decorated at neck and cuffs with bits of lace apparently meant to be white. She had come without the baby and after letting go the doorknob had lifted both arms to hold them tight across her breasts, hugging herself, as I had seen her doing the night before.

'Any tea?'

'The pot's still hot,' I said. 'But it'll be strong. I'll make fresh.'

She came over to the table as I got up from it to set her a place.

'Cornflakes?'

'God, no.'

'Toast, then?'

'No.'

When I had brought cup and plates to the table I said: 'You can't run around this house in bare feet. We don't have heated floors like those chalets.'

'I've noticed.'

She had sat down and was staring at the scrubbed boards.

'I can't stay,' she said. 'What I said last night about paying . . . I've no money.'

'You've been paid for.'

She looked up, but not really in surprise.

'Dean?'

I nodded.

'We met this morning. Out on the road.'

It was a moment before she asked: 'How long did he pay for?'

'Until he gets back.'

I thought she was going to ask how much, but she didn't.

'I won't be here that long. Nothing like it.'

If she had no money and was planning to leave 'Morvern' before Dean came in from his oil rig it could only be because she was counting on Murdo Menzies as her new protector. I could have told her that Murdo, nobody's Galahad, was sometimes away for weeks. He was missing for nearly two months when he got the Gain Estates head keeper's daughter pregnant, rejoining us with a deep sunburn and all ready to defend himself against the paternity suit that was never brought. It was said that he'd had a good time in Malta. I used to see the poor girl in the village, swollen from Murdo and hating life because of this. She had the baby at the Elsie Strang Memorial Maternity Pavilion just outside Taybridge, but gave it for adoption and then flew to California as a children's nurse to a Hollywood executive.

I had poured the girl's tea but she hadn't touched it. The top of my kitchen table seemed to fascinate her.

'About last night. It's like I said. I don't really take it.'

It is irritating to be treated as a fool. I took a deep breath.

'Look, Miss or Mrs whatever your last name is . . .'

'Hillis,' she said.

'Miss?'

'Yes.'

'Miss Hillis, you are now a lodger, as you called it, in my house. Paid for. Whether or not you use drugs is none of my business. Just so long as you don't use them *here*. When you leave you can have your box back. Meantime you'll have full board, including a midday meal. I'll put on the drawing-room fire if you want it, but it doesn't heat the place quickly and I think you'd be best in my back sitting-room. As you can see, I've lit the range here. The water ought to be hot enough to give the baby his bath in about an hour.'

The phone rang in the hall. I went to it, closing the kitchen door behind me. It was a man's voice at the other end of the line, not one I recognized, which made it a considerable surprise to be called by my first name.

'Sophia? Sophia McLinn?'

'Yes. Miss McLinn speaking. Who is that?'

'Geoffrey. Geoffrey Connors.'

I was about to say that I didn't know anyone by that name, then stopped in time. I haven't had so many proposals of marriage that I have forgotten the offers made, apparently in all seriousness, at the time, two to be precise. I was hoping that John would make it three, foolishly as it turned out.

'Oh,' I said. 'Geoffrey. How extraordinary!'

There was nothing extraordinary about it, really, Geoffrey hadn't flung off to Tanganyika after being spurned by me to forget the past on dangerous safaris, choosing instead to continue living in Edinburgh as a civil servant, looking forward to an index-linked pension as his comfort to the very edge of eternity. We had lost touch quite soon, though I heard somewhere only a few years ago that he had climbed relatively high in his profession, becoming a second under-secretary or something of the kind at the Scottish Office. I could remember that I had received an invitation to his wedding, but didn't go, sending two dish towels as a reminder of what might have been. What I said over the phone was what we all say when we are cornered by a voice from the past which we really have no wish to hear again.

'Where are you?'

The words weren't out of my mouth before intuition gave me the answer. He was at the Loch Riddoch Hotel enjoying one of their bargain winter break weekends. He was.

'I would so much like to see you again, Sophia. I only arrived last night. I was wondering about dinner here tomorrow? Would you come?'

I stalled on that one, trying to think of his wife's name in order to ask politely after her. It had been something very plain Scots like Jessie or Nellie, but before I could decide on anything he came to the rescue.

'You'll have seen about Elspeth?'

'What? No. I'm afraid . . .'

'You don't get the *Scotsman* these days?'

'Well, no.'

'She passed away. Just two months ago.'

I'm not sure that I said what one ought to a recent widower now enjoying a bargain weekend break, but he volunteered that he had come to Loch Riddoch even at this time of year because it was a place full of happy associations for him from long ago. It seemed that Elspeth had never liked the Highlands, so they had always taken their holidays in England, usually at Harrogate, though every third year they had gone to Scarborough to bring variety into their patterns. The wild adventure of a Mediterranean cruise had not been a success; Elspeth didn't like the heat and she got Continental tummy. We spent twenty minutes on the phone briefing each other on vanished years, or rather Geoffrey briefed me on *his* vanished years since I really had nothing to tell him beyond the fact that when Mother died, instead of cutting loose and going to Tahiti, I had turned 'Morvern' into a guest-house. This didn't seem to surprise him at all. I had been hoping it would.

My twelve-year-old Austin isn't the kind of car you often see parked in front of the Loch Riddoch Hotel and Chalet Complex; the cleaning staff have much newer models. Once the establishment had a certain charm, a bulky, late Victorian building, its public rooms furnished with mahogany and struggling palms in Chinese pots. Upstairs there had been two bathrooms per floor, one at each end, and huge, lofty-ceilinged bedchambers in which there was no heating of any kind and none expected, you were lucky if what came out of the hot tap at the basin was even warm. We used to stay there when I was a child while our maids, brought from Edinburgh, were opening up and airing 'Morvern', and I remember long meals starting with brown soup, then watery fish under a flour sauce, followed by boiled mutton and stewed cabbage, the whole topped off by a choice of two kinds of pudding, both heavy. I loved those meals, and so did brother Georgie. There was an old waiter who used to give us both the puddings with extra dollops of custard sauce, though this was strictly against the rules.

I got out of the Austin specifically worried about my fingernails after having been more generally worried about my overall appearance while I was dressing. I had broken two nails cleaning the flues on the range and a repair job with a file before cover-up with lacquer didn't disguise the fact that I now had the kind of hands that no one was ever going to think belonged to a concert pianist. My face had been treated to a second trial of one of those unbelievably expensive hormone creams which don't claim a permanent effect, only promising a return to youth for a matter of hours. I had bought the pot years ago in Perth in a moment of utter madness just after also going as far towards a holiday in Madeira as bringing home the brochures from a travel agent. Applying the cream according to instructions hadn't really whisked away the marks of a good few decades of living, though I was conscious of a certain tightening of the skin which probably could have been achieved just as well with white of egg. When young I had a good skin and what used to be called natural colouring, quite often going around with nothing more on my face than a touch of lipstick. Now I can never seem to get one with the right tone, they all seem too vivid, even a pale pink vivid, commenting almost savagely on my bid to be something I'm not and really never was. Also, I seem to be disadvantaged by my dressing-table mirror. This is placed where it should have a good light from the window, but I get up from the stool thinking that I'm quite presentable for a shopping trip to

Taybridge and then, in the town, see myself in shop mirrors with something of a shock.

The mirrors in the revamped Loch Riddoch hotel are pink to flatter the kind of guests who have lost youth while fighting for money. I went through the revolving doors on to thick carpeting laid over the old coloured tiles and those reflections said that hard work had helped me keep my figure, this better now than at eighteen when I was out in the world of Edinburgh semi-high society with a fair amount of puppy fat still clinging to my bones. My dress was a ten-year-old, but unlike most that you pay far too much for I hadn't gone off it, probably because it got worn so rarely.

Geoffrey had said he would meet me in the cocktail bar. An illumined sign lured me towards what had been the billiard room in my parents' time. It was now black leather, red lights, piped musak and very dim except for the white glitter on rows of bottles. You advanced on half-hidden faces, moving to a wordless, muffled tune on never-ending soundtrack. Half way to the bar counter I stopped, took a deep breath and stood wondering which of the males up on those stools could possibly be Geoffrey.

I should have guessed that he would never be up on any stool. He rose from a black settee and came towards me, identifiable because he had always been on the short side and this man was. Even when we stood opposite each other I couldn't really see his face. It was a bit like meeting an old acquaintance in the foyer to Hades, with a suggestion of fire and vague shapes all around, you another of them. We went towards the black sofa and sat on it, side by side, and almost immediately a waitress appeared.

In spite of the reddish tint all over her I recognized Edna, a village girl who worked as an assorted stand-in, sometimes as afternoon assistant to Willie the Shop, occasionally in the post-office fancy goods section, and now and again for me during one of those summer emergencies when Maureen, my regular help, was seized by one of her painful periods which made it impossible for her to get out of bed. In the last two years, however, I hadn't seen much of Edna, her rate per hour had zoomed and she had up-graded herself professionally to this kind of work. I didn't think the costume for the job suited her too well, a small cap perched on hair frizzed in a Taybridge salon, a mini apron above a flared mini skirt which left a large display of non-chorus-line legs covered in what seemed to be black fishnet.

'Hello,' I said.

' 'Evening, miss.'

In her night life she was pert. In the post-office or at 'Morvern' I would have been Miss McLinn.

I thought Geoffrey was a little surprised that it was whisky I wanted, and while he was ordering — a dry sherry for himself — I had a good look sideways at his face. The blueprint of the boy I could now remember was there. He didn't seem to have put on much weight, there was just a considerable sagging and what hair he had left was clearly white though now with that curious rouged look from the lighting. I was still checking up on him when he turned to do the same to me and for a good half minute we stared at each other, like a couple of mesmerists in contest. I had the feeling that this could go on indefinitely, so laughed to break the spell.

He said: 'You haven't changed much.'

He could have left off that 'much', but it wouldn't have been honest, and I was beginning to recall Geoffrey as a very honest boy always, something that must have served him well in the civil service.

'After all this time,' he said.

'Yes.'

I was glad when Edna brought me my whisky. She had made it a double without being told to, something

Geoffrey noticed as he was paying, a certain reluctance about putting down another pound note.

I needn't have bothered to give thought to what we would talk about, as I dressed preparing a suitable list of do-you-remembers from the yesteryears. It wasn't those years that interested him at all; he didn't want to be reminded of pimply youth, and before I'd had two sips of my whisky it was perfectly plain that Geoffrey wasn't one of those grey, self-effacing civil servants working tirelessly behind a screen of no publicity. Instead he had been in the vanguard of the new breed who don't believe in hiding their lights. He had retired at sixty with the splendid knowledge that the area of Scottish affairs he had in the end come to administer couldn't possibly have been handled better by anyone else. This must be a lovely thought to retire with, along with the high honour of having been made a Companion of the Bath, and should have guaranteed Geoffrey total peace of mind for the next decade or more, but there is a fly in every ointment. He asked if I would like another drink, not expecting me to say yes, but when I did he broke with a long tradition and had a second sherry himself. This seemed to burn a hole in whatever reticence he might have had normally in discussing his private life. The fly in his ointment had been Elspeth.

He didn't come anywhere near to saying that, in fact served me a long list of his deceased wife's good qualities, all of these dullish, and only when a picture had been established to his liking did he venture to suggest that the lady had been perhaps a shade too cautious in her approach to the recreational side of living. For instance, his idea of a retiral present to himself had been a three-months round-the-world cruise, but Elspeth had thought that was far too long to be seasick. He then suggested a winter in Florida, but she suppressed that by reading out pieces from the paper about muggings. Finally he had come up with the really revolutionary idea of uprooting from their terrace house in South Edinburgh and moving to a more exotic Scottish locale like Pitlochry or Oban, but the mere thought of this had plunged the lady into deep gloom.

We had a bottle of wine for dinner, one up from the cheapest on the list, Geoffrey choosing this carefully, taking so long over the performance that I could see him sitting in his government office in Edinburgh, with a red pencil handy, ready to score out what he thought were too extravagant items of projected public expenditure. The lighting was much better in the dining-room, letting us see each other properly, which ought to have been more discouraging than it was, at least from my side. He really wasn't at all badly preserved, and from the accidental contact of our knees under the table once or twice I got the impression that he was paying me a similar compliment. It was probably the Algerian plonk on top of two whiskies which seemed to propel me back, in more than just hazy recollection, to other little dinners in a blacked-out London, often to the sound of bombs louder than the music, and with the uniformed man across the table working away at his single purpose which was to steer me, at a not much later stage in the evening, to the room he had got for the night in the Grand Palace Hotel.

The prime Angus *filet à la Niçoise,* whatever that might mean, not properly de-frosted before cooked, was a lot tougher to chew than the old boiled mutton would have been. About all it did for me as a gastronomic experience was serve as a reminder that it was time I saw my dentist again. Geoffrey, who had given up his own teeth in favour of more durable porcelain, seemed to be having some trouble, too, so we didn't talk too much during that course, only really relaxing when we reached the stage of gâteau for him and cheese for me. It was then he told me about Oban, a man on the verge of living his dream.

I don't know how soon after Elspeth's funeral he had got in his car and driven to the West Coast to look at some bungalows being built on a hill behind Argyll's chief town, but it couldn't have been long. And once out there he had surrendered to temptation, impulse-buying one of the houses which didn't even have its roof on. This was rationalized afterwards as a logical enough step, the Edinburgh place now far too large and so on, but the whole project still remained a dramatic change of course in his living patterns, something very near to a completely new start. Beneath the man of the world who sniffed a bad wine for its bouquet, and then passed it as quaffable, was the boy at heart, eager and on tiptoe for moving day which couldn't happen for some time yet because the plaster in his new home needed time to dry out. He was stepping into the future with practically no impedimenta from the past, all the Edinburgh furniture to go to the salerooms while he spent a major portion of his retiral golden handshake on long-coveted antiques.

There was something almost endearing about Geoffrey detailing the delights of living in Oban, none of which he had yet experienced. He said that it was the kind of place where, if you got bored with routine, you simply went down to the big main pier and got on one of the mini-liners on the outer islands run. The islands were named for me, one after the other, with careful attention to the proper Gaelic pronunciation, the nearest thing to a poem one could expect from a retired top administrator. I listened with my elbows on the table and my hands folded under my chin, gazing across at him. I don't think he had had an audience like me for a good many years, and a sudden appreciation of this made him stop in the middle of a sentence about the golden beaches of Tiree to call the waiter and order two brandies.

I should have been fortified by then for what happened next, a mass descent on the dining-room of the young, eight of them, obviously straight here from a very good party up in one of the chalets. Two of the girls were almost beautiful and the other two moved in a way which said they gave what they had to offer so freely that you had no right to expect good looks as well. The males were in their twenties but somehow suggested schoolboys who had been seduced too early and were being loud to cover a secret shame over this. The newcomers moved to a big, round table and were at once central to the room, as though a spotlight had been turned on them, leaving the rest of the diners a fringe to be ignored.

Geoffrey patted his lips with a napkin.

'We'll have that brandy in the lounge,' he said. 'With our coffee.'

I went to the Ladies Room. This had been done up with a fitted carpet and a row of vanitory units. Standing by one of them, leaning over the basin being sick, was Edna. Her waitress's cap was sitting under the mirror. It looked as if it had been crushed in her hand. She turned at the sound of her name. She had been crying as well as vomiting.

'Oh! Miss McLinn . . . !'

'Edna, what is it? What's happened?'

She made a gulping sound in her throat, then swallowed and seemed to gasp for breath.

'Murdo . . .'

I went over to her. Her face was pitiful. She looked years older than I knew she was. Another of Murdo's girls. I hadn't heard about this one, but then in the winter, when Maureen doesn't come to 'Morvern', a lot of things happen in the village I don't get to hear about.

'Something's happened to Murdo?'

Edna nodded. She had turned and was sagging back against the vanitory unit. Her breathing was quick and shallow, as though pushed to this by a speeding heart.

'The police has just been,' she said. 'To the kitchens. And the main bar. Looking for Jock the garage.'

'Why?'

'I dunno. He was a pal of Murdo's.'

'Who is *dead*?'

'Aye!'

That came out as a wail.

'Do you know when it happened?'

'No. But they took him out the loch. Drowned. The police is asking questions. I don't know what about. I didn't stay. I had to come . . . here.'

She paused, lifting that crumpled face to look at me.

'He was my man, Miss McLinn! He was *my* man!'

It seemed unlikely that Murdo would have confirmed her claim.

CHAPTER 4

I had to go the hotel kitchens to get a cup of tea for Edna, who had started the kind of steady, quiet snivelling which must be stopped by something and tea seemed a better idea than slapping her. By the time I got back to Geoffrey he looked like a man about to organize a search-party. His reproof was almost falsetto.

'I thought you must have gone home!'

I put him in the picture, but since he had never heard about Murdo he couldn't work up much interest in our local tragedy, if indeed it could be called that. Also, having paid for my dinner, not to mention double whiskies and brandy, he felt I owed him my attention to *his* life. With the cost of eating out these days he had a real point there, but somehow I couldn't make a job of pretending a renewed interest in his Oban project. For a reason I wasn't going to try to analyse Murdo's death had spoiled any slight vicarious pleasure I might have got from sharing Geoffrey's dream. Its realization now seemed not even remotely possible. He had bought that house and he would go on to furnish it with his antiques, and in the few rationed sunny mornings out West he would stand on his new patio to look at the view across water to Mull. Slowly, or perhaps not so slowly, he would come to hate what he saw. He would get on those ships and go to the islands, landing on them when the spring flowers were flamboyant, seven different colours of wild orchis each surrounded by their courts of commoner blooms. And all that would mean nothing.

Geoffrey could scarcely help sensing the big switch-off from me, our contact sagging into the kind of doldrums that can happen after too much wine with a bad meal, words not just ceasing to flow, they had to be pried out in jerks the way you jack up a car, and as hard work. I had to fight not to look at my watch too soon for decency, keeping at bay the phrase about it being past the bedtime of someone who, in her mature years, had become an early night girl. In near-desperation I decided to try to make use of him, suggesting that he go to the public bar from which, even in the refined atmosphere of the lounge, we could hear sounds coming that might almost have been from a Gaelic uprising against the English oppressor. Geoffrey stared at me in total astonishment.

'What on earth *for*, Sophia?'

I tried to make it sound brisk and reasonable.

'Well, I couldn't get much sense out of Edna.'

'Sense about *what*?'

'Murdo's death?'

'And what has this man's death got to do with me?'

'Geoffrey, I just thought that you'd be able to get the story in the bar, that's all.'

'You want me to go to the public bar to ask questions

about a man I didn't know existed until this evening?'

'Not ask questions. Just listen. Over a glass of beer, you know.'

'Beer gives me flatulence.'

'Sorry. Skip the whole thing. It was a silly idea.'

I asked him if he had a second bathroom in the Oban bungalow and he wondered, more than slightly sullen, why on earth I was concerned about that? I wasn't, but I said that everyone seemed to be terribly bathroom conscious these days and that over the last ten years there must have been millions of new bathrooms installed in Britain alone and that I wished I had bought some plumbing shares with the three hundred and fifty pounds my mother's sister had left me nine years ago. By this time Geoffrey was staring at me with some concern.

'Are you upset about something, Sophia?'

'No.'

'It's having to deal with that hysterical waitress.'

'*No!*'

'If that's what you want I'll go to the public bar. What's this man's name again?'

'Murdo Menzies. But it's a silly idea, Geoffrey. Please forget about it.'

'I'll go,' he said, getting up.

He was away longer than I had been with Edna, returning to the lounge looking almost cheerful and with the kind of pink flush in his cheeks which beer doesn't give anyone except, I believe, the Japanese. As he settled I got a whiff of what he had been drinking.

'Packed in there,' he said. 'And hot. Isn't there a pub in the village still?'

'Yes. But they tell me the trade's moved up here.'

'I could see that. There must be a lot of drunken driving on these roads.'

'We've had three cars in the loch since last summer, and none of them tourists.'

'I'm not surprised. There wasn't a woman in that bar. Still cling to the old Scots traditions in Loch Riddoch, do we?'

'Except on Saturday nights. How do they think Murdo died?'

'What? Oh. Fell off a rock. Somewhere along the south shore road. Apparently there's a high bit where you can get a good cast. He used the place often. Seems to have been a keen fisherman. They think he slipped and must have hit his head. Then rolled into the water. Drowned unconscious. Something like that anyway.'

'Is that what the police are saying?'

'Just bar talk, I'd imagine. The police won't be saying anything yet. They only got the body out just before dark.'

'Where?'

'Some bit of shore just below where that side road over the Ben Tala hump branches off from the south shore loch road.'

Geoffrey was quite good as a private enquiry agent. It might be from his training at keeping a discreet check on juniors in his department.

'Know where that is?' he asked.

I knew all right. The cobbled beach is less than a mile from 'Morvern'. Two bodies from a boating accident were washed up there four or five years ago. There are currents in the loch which tend to carry everything down towards the village end of it, probably something to do with the river Tala outflow.

Geoffrey walked with me to my car. It was surprisingly mild, little wind where we were sheltered by buildings and the lochside trees, but high up the clouds were scudding, moonlight like a lamp being switched on and off. In the switch-offs Ben Tala was a looming bulk, suggesting the sinister volcano it once was.

'Beautiful,' Geoffrey said. 'It's a lovely valley.'

Beautiful, but it could be frightening, too. There are times in Glen Riddoch when the irrational seems to take positive shapes that multiply, forming weird regiments for an assault on reason. I never go for night walks in this place, even on clear moonlight nights, even when I had a dog.

'When am I going to see you again, Sophia?'

I looked up through the open car window.

'I don't know. How long are you staying?'

'I can stay as long as I like,' he said.

The terrible freedom. How he was going to come to hate it, every damn ticking minute. We were born to be slaves.

'Phone me,' I said, switching on the engine.

In the rear-view mirror I saw him standing looking after my car, the brightness of the glowing building behind, but before the Austin had reached the turn to the road along the lochside he had gone into the hotel. They have colour television in all the bedrooms now, waiting for you when you go up alone.

I didn't want to go back to 'Morvern', it was too early; Aline might still be about. If I had to be the one to tell her about Murdo the morning would be time enough. His death might mean nothing to her, it might mean a good deal; I had no way of knowing. Murdo could have been nothing more than a chance to escape from thralldom to her American. Dean loved the girl, or thought he did. I saw him again standing by the side of a road pointing to his heart. It was my guess, after only two contacts, that to someone like him love was being subpoenaed for total responsibility.

I turned the car away from the village, pointing it west along the north shore of the loch, a road winding in and out through a stunted forest of silver birches the western winds keep from ever reaching great height. The trees have adapted with squat, lichened trunks, clinging to slopes in a stony valley like mussels to rocks. It is a tricky road to drive even in daylight and at night becomes a dark obstacle course studded with sharp-angled bends and narrow stone bridges. In winter there are no lit windows, the few cottages along the road itself now summer places, and the occasional farm houses are hidden back in private glens. The local mansion, Riddoch House, is dark too, the laird, Colin Gain, leaving for his villa on Rhodes at the end of the grouse-shooting and not appearing in these parts again until the following May.

Normally I'm quite a fast driver, but I took this road at very moderate speed, thinking about Murdo Menzies. When the autopsy was over, and the police had released the body, the church bell wouldn't be long in ringing for his funeral. Donne claims that the sound of that bell, also tolling for me, ought to see me diminished in myself, but I couldn't feel that in this case it would. Nor, from what I had heard, would it diminish many in Loch Riddoch village. None the less, our local Don Juan would be given the usual send-off awarded to both saints and sinners, and all between, a blackcoated processional to the churchyard where the coffin bearers would be rewarded with a double whisky. These days, in the Highlands, women are permitted to attend burials, but few do, they still stay at home getting the funeral tea ready. To go would mean facing up to a masculine resentment almost as sour as Ladies' Day at what used to be an all-male golf club. The only women likely to be seen tagging along at the end of the column are almost certain to be relations over from the States wearing sunglasses, attending this still surviving local ritual as a good story for the neighbours when they get back to Chicago.

Most of us go through a kind of performance to the dead we have known, as though forced by that departure from life to assess what the relationship had meant. In

Murdo's case I knew all too well what it had meant. The chemistry between us had often been very positive, with moments when it had surged up to near-loathing, from his side as well. As a boy in the village, prone to games like laying down a breadcrumb trail, then shooting the birds one by one with an airgun as they landed to eat, he had maddened me to the point where I wanted to attack him with a knobkerry. Instead I had done my good citizen's duty and made my protest to the local policeman, which meant that the boy wasn't even reproved. Our constable and Willie the Shop are drinking pals, and it seems probable that when Murdo, aged eleven, was alleged to have put out the eyes of someone's pet rabbit, the boy's father and our representative of the law had a whisky together, agreeing to forget the whole thing.

I know that these seem tiny cruelties in a world burdened by vast ones, but they were cruelties within the orbit of my living, and almost under my eyes, and I raged at them, I couldn't help myself. And as I drove towards the west end of the loch, in and out of patches of light from a frightened moon and from tree shade, it still wasn't possible to dismiss certain recollections of Murdo by sanctifying these with a generous obituary. I don't have that kind of generosity and really don't wish to.

A light was the last thing I expected to see where the trees began to thin out for parkland in front of Riddoch House. It seemed too near the road to be from the mansion itself, but with the Austin swinging in and out of bends it was some time before I realized that the light was moving too, a car coming down the drive from what should have been a shuttered and deserted building. My first thought was burglars leaving with their loot, probably bitterly disappointed, for immediately after his mother's death Colin Gain had sent everything saleable to auction and built his villa on Rhodes from the proceeds.

The idea of Gain property being burgled didn't worry me in the slightest; what did was the likelihood that I was going to meet the criminal's car just as it was about to turn out of the estate into the road I was using. We get some rum customers in these parts, their prime targets the big country places which may still contain Chinoisery stolen from Peking during the Boxer Uprising, or pieces of the kind of furniture which continues to fetch high prices over in the States. I'm told these types usually travel with a large removal van at no great distance behind the command Jaguar, and I was looking somewhat anxiously for a second set of moving lights when the first lot went out.

I didn't care for that. I was certain that the car hadn't turned into the road to go west, or east to meet me, for either way I would have seen a flickering of light up in tree branches. Instead there was total darkness ahead, the moon in hiding. At the back of my mind had been the idea that I would turn the car at the Riddoch House gates. There aren't many places on a narrow, cambered road where you can do this, especially in an aged, outsize Austin which hasn't a remarkable turning circle.

The gates, like the house a half mile up the drive, are mid-Victorian and pompous about the money spent to build them, fat round stone columns surmounted by chipped griffins. When I was a girl the wrought-ironwork between the pillars had been closed every night by an under-gardener, but in a burst of patriotism during World War Two Mrs Gain had contributed this as scrap to help defeat Hitler and preserve us all from the sound of jackboots in Glen Riddoch. You come on those gates suddenly, after one of the S-bends featured on this road, car lights splashing over them. The Austin's lights did more than that, they splashed over a car stopped in the driveway, both sides and heads switched off, apparently waiting for me to go by and hoping not to be noticed while I did. What the driver hadn't been expecting was a really bright glare over him from my first new battery in three years. Whiteness picked him out even though he was on the other side of the car from me. He brought up a hand to shield his face, but too late. It was Colin Gain. I doubted that later, but not then.

There was now no question of turning. I drove on, conscious of an increased heartbeat for no sensible reason. If it had been Colin, I had seen him in his own driveway in his own car. Then I knew it hadn't been his own car, something much smaller, a Ford Escort perhaps. Colin advertised his presence amongst us again by appearing in one of the large BMW's, sand-coloured, and polished to glitter like gold. There was a kind of glitter about the man himself which made his emergence from this vehicle no anti-climax. At fifty he still retained traces of what had once been almost startling male beauty, the kind of head and carriage which, pictured in a glossy magazine, suggests generations of careful breeding to maintain the features of an artistocratic line. In fact Colin's great-grandfather had been a Midlands ironmaster who had taken over the foundry to which he was apprenticed and by middle age had made most of the million his descendents used to buy themselves blue blood status. There is no portrait of the money-maker hanging in Riddoch House, at least if there is I never saw it, and old Mrs Gain's idea of the way to entertain tea guests was to take them on a conducted tour of the vast building followed by the same of a vast walled garden.

A good half mile down the road beyond those griffins I still felt an unease, almost as if I was expecting a sudden flare of headlights behind the Austin that could mean a pursuit. Colin might be half drunk, the ex-rally-driver out for sport as a diversion from the utter boredom of having to come back to Loch Riddoch in winter on some matter of estate business. His parties on Rhodes were rumoured to be wild enough.

I decided to go home by the head of the loch, then around to 'Morvern' by the south shore road. It was miles out of my way and a waste of petrol, but I was going that route from a kind of funk I refused to admit to myself. I kept the car at a fair speed on the ever repeating bends, driving with what I knew of the Gain family very much at the front of my mind.

I didn't know them well. Mother would have said that she did, but this was nonsense, you never know your local royal family well, you are condescended to according to your placing on the various social levels beneath them. Because my father had been a surgeon who missed a knighthood by failing to be called in to attend the late Queen Mary during her summers at Balmoral, we rated well below the established county families but decidedly above the village general practioner whose wife only got asked to tea at Riddoch House once a year. Mother was invited twice, during July and August. Also, Mrs Gain came to tea with *us*. She had never been in the local doctor's house, explaining to my parents that such a visit might have caused talk in the village, which would never do.

Mrs Gain really ought to have been a Duchess, she had all the qualifications, confident that God had put her where she found herself in life, and that by entertaining the right people at the right time and in the right manner she was in some way fulfilling her part in His mysterious purpose. After Father's death and our move to live in 'Morvern' the year round my mother made the mistake of hoping to establish a greater degree of intimacy with the old lady of Riddoch House, forgetting that as a widow she had automatically lost status. It was actually quite a struggle to hang on to those bi-annual tea parties, and though Mother managed to do this, her only other chance to get past the griffin gates was at the Gains' annual garden fête. To attend this would have meant mixing with *hoi polloi* who were there to have their money taken off them to help support the Episcopal Church of Scotland. My mother was never seen at one of the fêtes.

Before the war I got taken to some of those Riddoch House tea-parties. It was always in summer, but I can remember the clammy cold of that drawing-room, clammier even than 'Morvern's' front hall. Though there is partial central heating installed now, our village carpenter tells me that there is dry rot throughout the fabric. Apparently the roof has nail sickness, with water getting in. He gives the place another fifteen years at the most before it will have to be blown up, one of those demolition jobs done for nothing as practice by Army engineers. We've seen quite a bit of this in our area, the Earl of Taybridge's castle is now a heap of stones in the middle of an overgrown meadow.

Colin Gain, however, is making pretty good use of the fifteen years left to his house, running it as a money-making proposition for people willing to pay huge sums for the privilege of shooting the Gain grouse. The place is really a hotel for four months in the year, with a chef imported from London and none of the staff recruited locally, this presumably to cut down on the gossip. The gossip still leaks out, talk of high old goings-on in the evenings, with a roulette table, and afterwards the paying guests accidentally on purpose finding their ways into bedrooms that aren't theirs. The grand old dame who watched over us all from the back seat of her ancient chauffeur-driven Daimler would be turning in her grave in the family mausoleum if Colin hadn't startled us all by having his mother cremated in Perth.

At the west end of the loch, set like a counterbalance to Loch Riddoch village, is a tiny hamlet, post-office-shop plus a handful of houses, and as I was passing through the place, where the windows were all dark, I knew that I had been a fool, allowing myself to be dictated to by something very near to panic. However, I had now turned east again, pointing towards home some ten miles away. Ahead, and after some open moorland, lay the Black Wood of Riddoch, which isn't nearly so sinister as it sounds, a long stretch of ancient pines, fat trunked giants that are direct descendants of a vast forest that in primeval times covered most of Scotland. In daylight I love the place, I go there for mushrooms and cones to soak in paraffin for firelighters, but at night it is certainly very dark, the trees almost roofing the road. It is a much better road than the one along the north shore by Riddoch House, wider, and with a surface renewed only years ago for the logging operations which still go on.

Before the forest there is a climb on to open moorland from which the view is splendid, and as I came up to the highest point the moon escaped from cloud, spotlighting the loch almost as far as the hotel complex and the village. Directly opposite, across water, Riddoch House, tall, turreted, and with shuttered windows, might almost have been an eccentric Victorian tombstone. Between the mansion and the hamlet I had just left were car lights going west at what seemed a much higher speed than my Austin, and I wasn't creeping. It was probably a wild boy hill farmer pushed out of the hotel bar at closing time now heading back for his glen and a long-suffering wife who would have tea waiting to sober him up. We have a few of these in the district.

The moon switched off as I reached the forest. It was a bit like entering one of those car tunnels in the Alps, headlights at first too bright for what they had to do, then the effect of them seeming to be absorbed by the walls, here trees, so that they became not quite bright enough. In the forest the road drops down to about sixty to a hundred feet above a cobble shoreline. Cliff-clinging pines continue to fence off the loch, but with breaks in that screen at promontories projecting out over the water. Some of these offer parking areas for cars and a few are equipped with picnic tables and benches. From the rocks on one of those points Murdo Menzies had fallen to his death.

I was taking one of the longest straights in the Black Wood, at just under sixty, when car lights came around a bend behind me. I was startled. No one lives anywhere along this stretch of road, foresters sometimes at work in the area all go home at night to a Norwegian timber village built half way to Taybridge. One hill farmer lives with his wife at the western edge of the forest, now miles behind me, and though Geordie McFie certainly drives as though all the roads in the district belonged to him I didn't think his battered Land-Rover would be capable of the speed of whatever was behind me.

The way those lights swelled was unnerving. My needle had gone up to sixty-one, very fast for an old Austin, but the driver behind was coming at near seventy, perhaps more. It wasn't the road for this kind of driving.

I braked down to fifty-five for a corner because I had to. Even then the car slewed getting around. There was another corner almost immediately. Before I had taken that the lights were a monstrous blossoming, flooding the inside of my car with a whiteness that almost gave me the feeling of being pushed forward towards the windscreen. If the driver behind wanted to know whether I was alone and a woman, he had certainly found out. A local would, by this time, have identified my car. I was certain it was a man in the driving seat, and highly skilled at what he was doing, following every manoeuvre I made tightly, keeping that dazzle light precisely where it would trouble me most. When I swerved his car stayed tucked in behind me, as though he had known what I was going to do before the idea came into my mind. I had flicked up the now useless driving mirror to eliminate the glitter from it, but my vision ahead was impaired by the terrible brightness inside the Austin. His car was so near mine that there was very little overspill from that concentration of light on to the road ahead and my own headlights, which I had thought so bright, now seemed almost dim. On bends they didn't have the strength to push in under the pines.

It came to me suddenly that I was the one setting the hectic pace. Risking the back end of my car, I braked hard. The Austin's tyres squealed. There was only the briefest waver of that white blast from behind, then it was back again full force. I wasn't bumped.

At forty miles an hour I had given myself a reprieve from total concentration on the road, mental space in which to try and find some reasonable explanation of what was happening. I didn't come up with much, except that this couldn't be some kind of game, unless it was a madman back there. He certainly wasn't drunk, no drunk could drive the way he was doing, with totally controlled precision. I tried to imagine what was in his mind, not making much of that.

Then suddenly I remembered what was ahead of us, at not much more than half a mile. The road climbs, then widens out at a break in trees on the loch side, and a sheer drop to a rocky shoreline. The road-widening had been to make space for parking by a dramatic view. Topping the cliff was nothing but a very low stone parapet as a base for wire interlock fencing. A car hitting this at anything like speed would go straight through.

I could still be going fast enough for his purpose. It wasn't easy to let that needle drop, thirty-five, thirty, twenty-eight. I seemed to be holding the car to a trundle.

As though I had spoiled his game for him, he gave it up. The dazzle glare seemed to be sucked back. When the Austin had rounded another bend the light had gone. I pulled down the driving mirror. The road behind stayed dark. I felt the victim of an hallucination.

It was now less than four miles to 'Morvern'. The Austin might be pushed to do sixty-five, though it was a long time since I had tried for that. I pressed down my foot. The engine coughed, then recovered. I tried a corner without any brake pressure and got a tail whip that was frightening. The road went up steeply and I came down a gear, the change noisy from too much speed for it. I was driving horribly and hated that. Large in my mind was the thought that this seeming escape was part of his game. In a much faster car he could now be following on dipped headlights, or just sides, keeping back until he knew I would be nearing the widened area above the cliff drop.

There was a glow ahead. Car lights came round a bend, a dazzle through my windscreen. I was going too fast for a twisting road and was too startled to dip. The other driver had. He blared his horn at me as we shaved past each other. He was right to. I braked down to careful motorist speed, pushing back a threatened panic.

I was safe now. Someone cursing me as he drove west was my guarantor of that.

CHAPTER 5

I was expecting the kitchen cooker to be out when I got home, but Aline must have added more fuel to keep herself comfortable, and the place was warm. She had heaped the dishes from her supper in the sink, but left them unwashed. I was expected to earn what Dean had paid me.

I made tea, poured a cup, then sat down at the table, determined to get back into the norm of my life quickly, and the first step towards this was to find a reasonable explanation for what had just happened, suppressing

imaginings. I could have been the victim of yobbos out
from Taybridge in a car looking for sport and finding a
lone woman to terrorize. I'm told it is called buzzing. It
certainly happens, though I haven't yet heard of it
happening in our area, even in summer with the caravan
site full. And yobbos would have been drinking. I was
sure the man behind me had been sober. I could see
Murdo Menzies playing this kind of game, and relishing
it, but unless someone had made a serious mistake he was
now in the police mortuary. I thought about possible
enemies, but couldn't come up with any very sinister
figure. The nearest to this were the village constable and
Jock the garage. The constable didn't care for me for a
number of reasons and Jock resented my total boycott of
his business, to the point where I never even got a nod
when we met in the High Street. Still, I couldn't see either
as the demon driver on a night road.

It was my good citizen's duty to go to the police about
the matter but even if I made my report to the district
headquarters in Taybridge our local man would be in the
picture at once. And I knew how he would react to that,
offering the village bar its big laugh of the week, if not the
month. I could hear the guffaws. That McLinn woman
out alone on the south shore road thinking the devil was
behind her. And she'd been drinking all night in the
hotel, too, before she caught sight of Old Nick driving a
Ford Fiesta. I was having none of that if I could help it.

I washed up Aline's dishes, found the water hot, so had
a bath and got to bed about one, expecting to spend the
small hours re-living my experience. Instead I slept at
once, and solidly, woken by bright light in my room. The
travelling clock said twenty past eight, which was late for
me even in winter, and by the time I got down to the
kitchen the nine o'clock radio news was saying that
another war was imminent in the Middle East. On the
kitchen table was a used cup and saucer, milk, sugar, a

cold teapot and an ashtray with four stubs in it, all of which seemed to suggest that Aline had got up very early indeed, something I wouldn't have thought likely, and had sat here a long time in a room still decidedly chilly because the stove draught doors hadn't been opened.

My next thought came almost as a hope. The girl had decided that 'Morvern' was no place for her, and had cleared out for good at first light. She could have been lying about having no money and there was certainly no sound from the room above. I went to the back door to find it still bolted, then down the hall to the front which had just been pulled to. I stood for a moment looking down the drive, almost seeing Aline, laden as she had arrived, and wearing that ridiculous hat, disappearing into the mists of dawn. Back again in the kitchen I wondered if I had been actively unkind to the girl. I can, on occasion, be quite grim over the business of getting an unwanted paying guest to move on, offering minimal landlady service, and no hint of a smile, but except for that business over the heroin I didn't think I had been like this with Aline; indeed, any bid to establish a workable relationship between us had come from my side. The most she had offered had been a kind of passive indifference.

When I heard the cry I thought at first it was from one of the seagulls which visit us in winter. Then I knew it was from the room above. I went up the back stairs, knocked, but didn't wait long before opening the door.

Aline hadn't left, at least not with her luggage. The gladstone bag was still in the middle of the floor and her baby in the middle of the bed. The child had kicked the quilt off and was lying with legs kneading the air, arms punching it. His crying wasn't steady, the sound let out when he had any breath to spare from a hard training session. In a cold room he was wearing only a nappy and my total lack of experience with babies didn't keep me from seeing that this needed changing.

Aline must have gone for a walk after smoking those four cigarettes down below, carrying on a brooding session out of doors. I didn't allow myself to look at even the fringe of an idea that she might have left 'Morvern', and her possessions, for a new life without the burden of them, including the burden of her child. I stared down at the baby and he stared up at me, now without making a sound, but still managing to put across the idea that he wanted that nappy changed, and at once.

It was something I had never done and never expected to have to do, but at one period my life had been dotted with semi-emergencies requiring instantaneous decisions, and I decided to take action on this one. There were fresh supplies of nappies . . . well, two . . . in the commode my mother had once decorated with medicine bottles and on the floor beside it was a bowl acquired without permission from my pantry. I took the bowl to the bathroom and returned with warm water and a washcloth, then proceeding on the principle learned in an Army vehicle maintenance course which is that before you start stripping anything down you memorize at each stage how it has been assembled. I noted the way the pins had been inserted and while removing the offending nappy itself committed to memory just where it had been folded. I was slow over the job, so slow that Pete showed signs of impatience at certain stages, though he didn't actually give voice to any loud complaints, just a sort of muttering. It was while I was applying a baby talcum to what seemed the necessary areas that I thought I heard voices in the front hall.

I couldn't remember whether I had locked the door down there, and was going to find out when there was a sound from directly beneath me, like a chair being dragged back over linoleum, followed by a mumble that could only be a man's voice. The only explanation seemed to be that Aline had brought someone back with her and was entertaining in my kitchen. The idea was preposterous. I wanted to go storming down the back stairs, but forced myself to go along to the bathroom with the washing bowl and used nappy. I had a look out of the upper hall window. Parked below was a white car making no pretence about not belonging to the police.

Pete couldn't be left lying on the bed wearing nothing but a clean nappy and a quilt put over him would just be kicked off. He had to be dressed in something. I didn't know where Aline kept his clean clothes, if there were any, so went into my own room to rummage through drawers, not knowing what I was looking for. An old grey cashmere cardigan felt soft enough and really before I realized what I was doing I had cut off the sleeves three inches from the shoulders and the buttons. I took a scarf and went back to the baby.

All the time I was fitting Pete into his makeshift kimono I heard the grumbling of voices from below, not just one male down there, but at least two. Much as I wanted to rush down for a confrontation I had to finish what I was doing, and this took time. Finally I stood and, looking down, used the voice that had always brought my dog to heel.

'You will now *sleep*!'

Pete smiled at me for the first time. I put the quilt over him. He allowed me to get to the door before letting out a shriek. It was a sound that should have brought the child's mother up the back stairs, but it didn't. I was feeling somewhat unnerved and it was a moment or two before I put out my hand to the knob for a second time. His reaction was lower pitched, the kind of yelling I believed he could keep up for a long time if necessary. And meant to. The only thing I could do was take him with me. I went back to the bed and picked him up. The yelling stopped. Swathed in cashmere, he made a relatively easy bundle to carry, though heavier than I was expecting.

On the uncarpeted back stairs I had to watch where I put my feet, which slowed down our progress and announced our imminent arrival. The mumble of voices died away. I was outside the door for a moment shifting the baby's weight to free a hand for that knob. Outraged I might be but I didn't achieve anything like a dignified entrance.

My kitchen appeared to have been converted into a police interrogation room. There were three men in there with Aline, who was seated alone at the table. All were looking at us. The men showed considerable surprise but the girl showed nothing.

One of the men was our local constable, the other I took to be a sergeant in the Taybridge force. The sergeant had a pad open on one knee and must have been writing in it somewhat awkwardly, as though it was a matter of policy not to share a table with the person being interrogated. And certainly Aline did seem to be laying a claim to my scrubbed boards, her arms out on them, as she leaned forward, an odd position, but which meant she could keep her head down when answering questions, if she *had* been answering them. The third man in the room looked as though he had been given intensive training in keeping himself inconspicuous, his chair pulled well back from that centrepiece of two policemen and the girl. He wore a grey suit, had pepper and salt hair, and gave the impression that he would be extremely tidy in everything he did.

The first words were spoken by me, but as I was shifting the baby's weight while I uttered they weren't as impressive-sounding as I had intended.

'May I ask what all this is about?'

Constable McWilliam had been staring at me, not quite open-mouthed, but still apparently astonished that

I was capable of holding a baby without dropping it. As he rose I saw his eyes glinting behind spectacles he would certainly immediately lose in any rumpus with a criminal, thus automatically rendered useless.

'Oh, Miss McLinn!' That was almost a shout. 'We met this young lady when she was out walking. Or I should say, was making her way to the hotel. Sergeant Johnson here had a few questions to ask her. We thought we'd better do it inside, you see. And not in the police station, as you'll understand.'

'No, I don't understand.'

'Well, we didn't want to make it official, like. That is, Sergeant Johnson didn't. He's from Taybridge. That gentlemen over there is Detective-Inspector Wilcott of . . . ah . . . a special branch, you might say.'

I thanked him for his introductions and then wanted to know, politely enough, on what authority the police were making use of my house without my permission. The constable said that the 'lassie' had brought them in. Before I could comment on that the sergeant looked up from his notes and said:

'Take a seat, Miss McLinn.'

That sounded very like an order. One of the things you have to learn to do in the Services is control personal anger. I managed this, but I hoped my voice was as icy as I intended it to be when I said that I must now riddle the ash from the cooker if I didn't want it to go out. I gave Pete to his mother, then did a thorough job on the stove before going to the sink to wash my hands. It was a good five minutes before I turned to look for a chair, not a word spoken during this time. I might have been a VIP for whom a performance was being held up.

The only unoccupied chair was over against a wall by the dresser. I sat there without moving it and from the sidelines was at once conscious of the formal arrangement at the centre of my kitchen, the Sergeant and Constable, with their backs to the range, in chairs neatly side by side directly facing the girl. Detective-Inspector Wilcott, obviously vastly senior to his colleagues, had established himself as a neutral to the proceedings, not a word out of him so far and from the looks of things none likely. From where I was he was cut off at upper chest level by the table, somehow suggesting a bust of one of the quieter Roman Emperors. He had looked at me when I came in with the baby, and probably while I was shaking ash out of the stove, but he wasn't doing it now, almost as though he had seen all he needed to come to a conclusion and file it.

The questioning of Aline was apparently over, it was to me the sergeant turned.

'Know anything about the drug heroin, Miss McLinn?'

I considered this, then said that all I knew was what I read in the papers.

'Does this mean you wouldn't recognize the signs of drug addiction?'

'I haven't the faintest idea what the signs are.'

Aline was now staring at the top of her baby's head.

'That means you wouldn't have known the lodger you took in some days ago is a heroin addict?'

'Of course I didn't know. Otherwise I wouldn't have let her past the door.'

'So when did you find out?'

'You've just told me, Sergeant.'

'You'd no inkling before?'

'How could I have?'

The policeman was making notes on the pad on his knee. He took a good two minutes at this, then looked back at me.

'The young lady has no objection to our searching her room. How do you feel about that?'

'Sergeant, when I rent a room it passes under the jurisdiction of the renter for the time being. If the girl doesn't mind by all means search her things. Her room is above this one. Use the back stair.'

'Is your meaning in that that we're not to search anywhere else in the house?'

'You will require a warrant,' I said.

The man who looked like one of the better class of Emperors was looking at me. Sergeant Johnson was back to his note-taking and without looking up from this he ordered McWilliam to search Aline's things, and the constable left us, not without a certain visible bitterness at being cut off from proceedings down here. His feet thumped on the bare wooden treads as he mounted aloft. Sergeant Johnson looked at me again.

'Before this young lady came to you as a lodger had you any knowledge of her?'

'None.'

'You hadn't heard any talk in the village about her? Or anything like that?'

'Not a word.'

'So you took someone in about whom you knew nothing? At a very late hour?'

'It depends on what you call a late hour.'

'We'll not quibble, Miss McLinn. You know very well what I mean. The constable tells me that you never take lodgers in the winter. And you never have babies here at any time. So wasn't it a bit of a queer thing to do, having this young lady in?'

'Yes,' I said.

He wrote that down.

'So why do it? I might ask what your motive was?'

'Humanity.'

He wrote that down, too. The Roman Emperor caught me looking at him and looked away. I wondered if he went through his professional life like this, with absolutely no comment on the situations in which he found himself.

'At the risk of sounding a wee bit offensive, Miss

McLinn, I'm going to suggest that maybe what you call your humanity could be out of character in your case.'

I had to admit it was a neat point. I smiled at him. His face offered no response to that.

'One does from time to time,' I said.

'One does *what*?'

'Act out of character.'

'I'm not with you?'

'I've just changed that baby's nappy, Sergeant. It's not a job I've ever done before or expect to do again. But I did it.'

As though to counter what she saw as a bid to turn attention back to her Aline suddenly concentrated on motherhood, unbuttoning her blouse and giving Pete her right breast. Sergeant Johnson, obviously a family man, didn't appear to notice but the gentleman called Wilcott was interested. The interrogation of me proceeded.

'I put it to you, Miss McLinn, that you took in this young lady because you were offered a large sum of money to do so?'

'Nonsense! I took her in because it was snowing. There was no question of money raised until the next morning. And then what you call a large sum was practically thrown at me by her young man.'

'Whom you had met by arrangement?'

'No, by accident. I was having a walk. Along the shore road to the village.'

'What time would it be?'

'Well, daylight on a fine winter's morning. Half past eight perhaps. On the whole I prefer Loch Riddoch when its inhabitants are still asleep. It was Sunday and they were. The young American was the only person about. On his way back to his oil rig. He threw the money at me because I had refused to take it.'

'You were going to keep this young lady for nothing?'

'No. I was going to put her out. It was no longer snowing.'

Mr Wilcott actually laughed. A little snort as he looked at my black range. Sergeant Johnson plodded on, determined.

'This money, large enough maybe to be a bribe, made you change your mind?'

'No one tries to bribe me, Sergeant. It was perhaps a generous amount for two weeks in my house. No more than that. About what you have to spend for a gala winter weekend at our hotel, use of sauna and heated swimming pool included.'

The exchange with Sergeant Johnson was coming to remind me of ping-pong at our Army recreation centre with my girls. This activity had been part of a directive from on high intended to increase officer/other-ranks off-duty contacts and thus improve corps morale. It hadn't worked, of course; the only way to improve corps morale in the Services is to tighten discipline. But while I was obliged to play those ridiculous games I played them to win, and win I did, this not because my girls let me.

The sergeant went off on a new tack.

'I understand from the constable, Miss McLinn, that you had dinner in the hotel last night?'

There is no such thing as a private life in the country. I nodded.

'So you'll have heard about this man Murdo Menzies being drowned, then?'

'Yes.'

I looked at Aline. She was looking over the baby's head towards the range. I was pretty sure the police had told her about Murdo's death, it would have come out in the questions asked her, but that couldn't have been as much as an hour ago. Her face showed nothing. If I hadn't taken that cigar box away from her I'd have said she was insulated against feeling by another dose of the drug.

'How well did you know this man Menzies?' the sergeant asked.

'Well, we weren't exactly friendly. Though I was very much aware of him. We all were in this village.'

'How do you mean?'

'Just conscious of him about. You couldn't help being. He was a vandal before vandalism was so generally fashionable. He was up before the magistrates in Taybridge a few times, but was just admonished. I don't believe his father ever had to pay a fine.'

Sergeant Johnson didn't put down my thoughts on Murdo, instead flipped back pages in a search for earlier notes. The mystery man called Wilcott had taken out a pipe and, seeing me looking at him, asked politely if I would mind the fumes. I told him to go right ahead. We exchanged smiles across the kitchen. The sergeant coughed, to bring me to heel.

'I see you reported him for poaching. The deceased, that is.'

'You have been well briefed on my past, Sergeant. Though I'm surprised Constable McWilliam brought up that little matter.'

'Why did you think he wouldn't?'

'Because he did nothing whatsoever about the evidence I gave him.'

'Just what was that evidence, Miss McLinn?'

'I saw Murdo coming out of woods fringing the north shore road carrying his gun and six or eight brace of grouse. It was a few days before the official opening of the season on the birds. What he meant to do was hang on to those grouse until it was time to ship them off to London as the year's first game. You get a fancy price from a top hotel if you win that race. I expect Murdo had been doing this ever since he was big enough to carry a gun.'

'Constable McWilliam states that Mr Gain of Loch Riddoch House refused to press charges.'

'Most charitable of our local laird,' I said.

'And when was all this?'

'Autumn two and a half years ago.'

'Your relations with the deceased have been strained ever since?'

'If you could call them relations they've been strained ever since he was about nine.'

There was a sound of feet descending the back stairs. The constable made his report from the doorway, semi-formal over it, going into considerable detail about how thoroughly he had searched the room above. He might almost have been expecting to be challenged on his qualifications as a sniffer out of hidden drugs. Then I realized that the performance was not for the benefit of Sergeant Johnson, but beamed towards the pipe-smoker, who was polite enough to nod appreciatively.

I can't claim that the questioning of me had turned out to be much of an ordeal and certainly I could make no complaints about police brutality. Sergeant Johnson indicated that our contact was about to end by very deliberately turning over the pages of his notebook until it offered a clean sheet for future memos. Then he pushed back his chair and stood. It was all rather oddly like the end to a dullish tea-party, everyone wanting the business over but without seeming to rush things. I went with them down the hall to the front door and as I opened this Mr Wilcott picked up his coat from a chair, giving me a bow and a smile as he passed. Not a man to throw unnecessary words about.

There was some banging of car doors, then they drove off, no one waving to me. I stood to see them out of the drive, then went straight to what used to be our drawing-room but is now referred to by my summer guests as 'the lounge'. In winter the fire is never on in there, but I like to think that it sits ready should a surprise social occasion occur, and in the late autumn I do a six months' flower arrangement of dried hydrangea blooms which sits on a gateleg table just beyond the front double windows. The fluted Chinese bowl holding the display doesn't have any water in it, just sponge plastic to hold the stems with paper beneath this. I lifted out the plastic and the paper without really disturbing the hydrangea arrangement. What I had put at the bottom of the bowl was no longer there. I put back the display, taking time to straighten a couple of stems, then went along to the kitchen.

Aline was still sitting at the table, apparently in one of those semi-trance states which some would probably label as meditation. While striving to attain inner peace she didn't seem to be holding her child very securely.

I said loudly: 'Where have you hidden it?'

She lifted her head. I think if she had pretended not to understand I would have become very angry, but she didn't try that on me.

'That big thing with the lid. Top shelf.'

The top shelf in the kitchen dish cupboard has always been dedicated to my mother's marriage dinner service, a hundred and twenty-four pieces now reduced to sixty-three and some of these cracked. Once a year I wash them all. The tureen is the surviving queen of what is usually a dusty display. I got up on a kitchen chair, as Aline must have done, to grope in under a lid, pulling out the cigar box. I got down off the chair and, without looking at the girl, went over to the cooker. Before she realized what I was going to do I had opened the fuelling door and pushed in the box.

Aline screamed. Pete, fallen to the floor, started to scream as well.

CHAPTER 6

The baby was half under the table. I had to go down on my knees to reach him. When I got up again, holding Pete, the girl was back in her chair, slumped in it this time, her eyes shut. I couldn't hear, over the howling of the child, whether she was making any kind of noise herself, though her lips were moving. I found myself doing what I had long ago seen Italian women doing with a baby in distress, giving it little pats on the back while jigging it up and down.

I suppose I must have looked ridiculous, but the jigging worked, there was suddenly silence in the kitchen. And the girl was now staring at me. It might have been that she was disgusted by the spectacle of me dancing around with her son in my arms. I stood very still, hating her, the feeling uncoiling in me like a snake waking to hunger. Holding Pete high against my body, his head almost over my shoulder, I went to a chair by the dresser, sitting there at the edge of my kitchen to see it from an angle that was strange. The stage set for my life had been usurped by a girl performing a stock role in one of those plays I read about in reviews, but never go to see, or watch on television. Any apparent flickers of sympathy between us had been an illusion, with her there could be no coming out from walled in self-attention.

Holding Pete, now apparently asleep, I thought about Dean, the tall boy as tightly trapped by his imagined love as I had been by my imagined duty to my mother. I had suddenly a sharp curiosity about him that made no sense from it roots in two brief meetings. I wanted to know how he could have stumbled into the situation that now had him gripped by octopus tentacles.

Aline got up from the table and crossed the kitchen to stand over us. The baby was now making small bubbling noises that must have been wind coming up behind schedule.

'Give him to me,' she said.

I don't know why I held on to the child.

'Give him!' she said again.

She would have reached down and torn the baby from me. Carefully I lifted him down from my shoulder. There was a short whimper during the transfer. Aline took Pete across the room and out by the door to the back stairs. I got up and went over to the stove, riddling it again. It is a waste of fuel to shake out the ashes too often, but I did it anyway. I wanted to hear a roaring in the chimney. I was still standing by the cooker, holding out to it hands that weren't cold, when the bell rang.

I went down the hall thinking it was the police back again, but it was Geoffrey. This morning he was very much a visitor from long-lost yesterdays. I had a job getting out the right words about a beautiful evening in his company. I asked him in for a coffee but he was on the way to Taybridge to shop.

'Don't you remember how we used to do this, Sophia? Call on neighbours to see if they wanted anything in town.'

'What?'

'I mean, back in those summers.'

'Oh.'

'You could come with me?'

I saw his car for the first time, a Metro, suitable for a man who has retired and doesn't want the world to get the impression that he is splashing out from the security of an income that will always swell to meet economic change.

'Not this morning, thanks.'

'Well, how about some messages? I'm used to shopping. Even in supermarkets. I used to do it quite a bit in

Edinburgh. Really to keep in touch.'

I didn't ask with what. To please him I ordered sugar and bacon, then kitchen soap. He had out a notebook and was writing things down carefully, as he would the prices later.

'I did enjoy last night, Sophia.'

'Yes. It was lovely.'

'I lay awake a long time in my room after the television programmes closed down. Thinking about the old days, you know. I hadn't thought I'd really remember them the way I am. I mean, in coming here.'

I said that he was making me remember them, too, though that wasn't quite the truth. He told me that Ben Tala had been looking beautiful when he woke up and somehow this had put him back all those years to being eighteen again, though he wasn't too happy about the hotel's Continental breakfast, they wouldn't serve bacon and eggs in the bedrooms. I couldn't really see the connection between being eighteen and bacon and eggs, but didn't ask for an explanation for fear I would get it at some length.

I asked him back to tea that afternoon and stood watching him go down to his car. He turned to wave, acknowledging my politeness. He couldn't have had the Metro for very long, making a mess of his gear changes in the drive. I stood there suddenly feeling as irritated by that as I used to when one of my girls abused the clutch on an Army vehicle.

Back in the kitchen I remembered that I had promised my paying guest full board. I am not a great cook, and, living where I do, don't find the raw material much of an inspiration. We get fish by van from Taybridge once a week which offers us filleted haddock that looks, and tastes, as though it had gone the round of the Aberdeen shops for a week before being sent out to us. It is much the same with the meat. These days no butcher's van comes near us, the Menzies' supermarket keeping a supply of aging cow and mutton in its cool cabinet, plus tinned mince waiting on the shelves. I could get away with cold Spam for lunch but if Aline was going to have a hot meal tonight an empty larder meant that I was going to have to pay a visit to the village shop. Since I hadn't been in the place for over two years my sudden appearance was going to be put down to an uncontrollable curiosity about the details of the finding of Murdo's body. However, when I got to the Menzies' establishment, at well after twelve, the matter appeared to have been talked out by the locals, the place empty of customers, everyone home warming up the pre-cooked tinned mince.

There had been great changes since I was last here, the shop updated to the latest thing in contemporary rural merchandising with a great deal of plastic and an electric fly catcher on the roof. There was even a bargain section on the shelving in which the prices were only twenty per cent above what I would have to pay in Taybridge, the big feature this week being dented tins of South African peaches. The sound of me picking up my basket reached the checkout girl as the squeaking of the door apparently hadn't. She turned. It was Edna.

Suffering had left traces in red eyes, but otherwise she looked far better groomed than I had ever seen her in daylight. I said I was surprised to find her here this morning and she said that you have to just carry on, don't you? There was then a lull while I inspected the canned soups until suddenly she informed me that she only worked here in the mornings.

'It passes the time, don't it? Not that old Menzies upstairs pays anything like the going rate for a half day. Still, it's a job. You're supposed to be thankful. I'll tell you this, if things wasn't so bad there I'd be off to Glasgow tomorrow. Or London.'

I moved on to the packaged cereals. There was a new one, semi-laxative, which might appeal to my summer guests.

'My Mam says it's a good thing,' Edna shouted. 'About Murdo and me, I mean. Mam hated me being out with him. There was rows when she knew I was. Mostly I didn't tell her. I mean, I'm twenty-three, Miss McLinn, even if I am living at home still. Where else is there to live in this dump?'

I certainly wasn't offering to have her live in at 'Morvern'. The subject required changing.

'I need some boiling beef, Edna. Where's the cool cabinet now?'

'Over beyond they veg racks. Enjoy your dinner at the hotel?'

'I've had better.'

'I can believe it. You should see in that kitchen. Some-body asks for something on that yard-long menu they wasn't expecting. Pierre, that's the chef, goes to the deep freeze but canny find the packet. You know where Pierre comes from? Dundee. Real name's Willie McKay. He was on the dole before he took up cooking. You should see what goes into his soup of the day for the bar lunches. Fair turns me stummick.'

I was now at the far end of the shop but her voice hunted me down.

'I heard all about your gentleman friend from the barman. He's got a new house in Oban. Going to live there, instead of Edinburgh.'

I didn't say anything.

'Used to come here when he was young. That when you knew him?'

I put back a tin of bargain baked beans.

'Yes.'

'I been in Oban. Two days. Rained all the time. What

you looking for now?'

'Baby food.'

'Eh?'

'There's a baby in my house at the moment.'

'*What*? I hadnae heard!'

'I haven't put up any notices about it.'

'But, Miss McLinn, how would *you* get a baby . . . ?'
She stopped. Her voice had been rich in disbelief.

'I have the baby's mother, too,' I said, still checking along the shelves.

There was quite a long pause, then Edna's voice, loud:
'You don't mean . . . ? Not that bitch? Not that Aline?'

I moved to where we could see each other. The pallor from last night's grief had gone, colour starting in two bright spots on her cheeks and spreading fast, already threatening her neck.

'You don't like her?'

My question was too abrupt. Softly, softly might have got me some way to a real answer, but it is not a skill I have handy. The girl sitting behind the cash register was suddenly seeing me again as the spinster who kept lodgers in a big, bleak house, almost as segregated from the wicked world as someone who has taken the vows of an enclosed order. What Edna allowed herself to say was cobbled together from stray thoughts left loose around the edges of her real feelings about Aline.

'Och, well, you know what I mean, Miss McLinn. I don't really like the way she carries on. They kaftans and all that.'

'Kaftans?'

'Aye. Used to come into the hotel bar wearing them. You could see there was nothing on underneath. And they was thin, too.'

Fishnet stockings were okay but kaftans without underwear were not allowed. Edna now wanted to close a topic threatening to become embarrassing.

'The baby food's along this side, Miss McLinn. My
Mam always used that Bayola on us kids. I was never
breast myself, just the bottle and Bayola. Went on it at
five months, Mam says. Brother Eddie was on it, too.'

Brother Eddie was six feet one and now in the
Manchester police force. I put the package in my basket.

'Instructions is on the pack,' Edna announced. 'Dead
easy. I mean, to mix up. Why, my Mam swore by it.
Nothing to do, really. She was never one for spending
herself on us, if you know what I mean?'

I knew what she meant. Edna's mother had spent a life
dedicated to squeezing the last available halfpenny out of
state security, operating this profession with marked
success even from the depths of the country. Edna's father
had disappeared from the scene long before I came to live
at Loch Riddoch, now nameless and never referred to, at
least not in my hearing.

I took my basket to the checkout.

'Ring up the Menzies ninety per cent profit on this,
Edna.'

'You can say that again. You know this, I never buy a
damn thing here. I don't let my Mam come in much
either. Fetch the stuff home from Taybridge. It pays the
bus twice over. That's when I don't get a lift.'

She stared at a wall.

'Mostly Murdo took me. Away from his Pa's shop. You
could say that was funny, I suppose.'

There were signs of grief returning.

'Funeral's day after tomorrow. At the cremmy in Perth.
I was going but I'm not now. It's too far. I suppose they
had to burn him. They say he was a horrible sight. The
police is saying he was in the water for near three weeks
and . . .'

'I'd rather you didn't tell me about it.'

'Och, sorry, Miss McLinn. It's just sitting here when the
shop's empty. You get to thinking.'

She took out a handkerchief and blew her nose. Then, after we had both given the memory of Murdo a half-minute silence, she recovered enough to punch buttons on the computerized accounting machine it was rumoured had cost Willie Menzies getting on for two thousand pounds. I suddenly remembered that I was out of ketchup and had gone back to the shelves when I turned to an uninterrupted view of both of the shop's two plate glass windows. Jock the garage's pickup van was in the street beyond, moving along very slowly in the direction of 'Morvern', with Jock himself clearly visible behind the wheel peering towards the Menzies emporium. For a man who normally drove at wild speeds his present eight miles an hour was in itself enough to stir curiosity and that, coupled with what seemed to be an intense interest in a shop he certainly saw many times a day, had me standing perfectly still holding my red bottle. I don't know whether he saw me doing this, but he suddenly accelerated away. I went back to the checkout to ask a leading question.

'How's Jock taking Murdo's death?'

Edna sniffed.

'Oh, *him*.'

'They were close friends.'

'Aye. And I couldn't stop it. It was something that started at the school. Like a lot of bad habits.'

'You don't like Jock?'

'I think he's rubbish. I know fine what it was with Murdo. He could make Jock do anything. Men like having a stooge. You see it all the time.'

'Never with women?' I asked, putting down my money.

She thought about that before punching the total button.

'Well, you don't see anyone following me around with her mouth open. Honest, it was like that dog Murdo had, you never got away from him. We'd go to the pictures in

Taybridge and when the lights came on there'd be Jock
three rows down turning his head to look back at us. He
gave me the creeps sometimes, I'm telling you. When I
said anything about it to Murdo he'd say shut up. Real
sharp, like.'

'Has Jock never gone with a girl?'

'Not that I know of. It's engines with him.'

She gave me my change. I went out into a street
absolutely deserted for a midday break more piously
observed than any of our Sundays, the post-office always
shut by half past twelve, and quite often fifteen minutes
before that. The twice daily bus from Taybridge arrived a
little after one, causing a slight flurry, but this dying
down quickly, closing front doors absorbing the travellers
even before the bus had done its ritual circling of the war
memorial and was starting back towards Taybridge
again, usually empty.

I was nearly at the humped stone bridge when the
sound of a car coming towards it from the other side
made me decide to wait on the grass verge, which was just
as well, for it was Geordie McFie, a hill farmer, in his
battered Land-Rover which he used like a tracked
vehicle, confident that if he had to he could knock the
competition clean off the road. The way he hit that bump
on the bridge was unnerving enough for me and might
have been part of a campaign to keep Scotland clear of
tourism. Also, he has a beard he grew because it was
easier than shaving, not even trimmed when they flew to
see their son in Toronto, and that hairy visage peering out
from behind a greasy windscreen might have been
calculated to strike fear into the hearts of the visiting
English.

He saw me and braked. This meant that the Land-
Rover slewed first in my direction, then away, before
coming to a halt.

'How are you then?' he bellowed. 'Haven't seen you

since we got back.'

'I'm as usual. How was Toronto?'

'It's all right for Tom, it wouldn't do for me. It's not sheep country round about. You know this, they never eat mutton. Never saw it on the table the whole time. My son's table at that. And him raised on these braes. And it was bloody cold. I'll never go there in the winter again. The wife liked it, though. The shops. I was going to ring you up. About a dog.'

I didn't say anything, very conscious of blue eyes peering at me from under untrimmed eyebrows.

'You remember what I said after what happened to your Chow? You ought to get another right away. I've not heard of you doing it.'

'No. I haven't.'

'Nearly six months, isn't it?'

'Not quite.'

'Well, I've got a dog for you. Bitch, rather.'

'No.'

'Listen to me, woman! The wife said you'd be like this. You remember our Nell pupped back in the summer? The dogs are all right, they'll train for the hill, but there was one bitch. She came into this world meaning to take it easy. Work? Not her, never.'

'If I wanted another dog it wouldn't be a bitch. And not a collie. I couldn't cope with one. Not the way I live.'

'You could cope with this collie. Fluffy is what the wife called her. You should see her. All charm. The wife doesn't want her away, but I've no room for play dogs. This one could be thinking she was born by the swimming pool of one of those Hollywood millionaires. Lies on her back with her legs straight in the air, laughing. I'll bring her round for you to have a look.'

'Please don't!'

'Like some eggs? You'll have to take them in a bag, I haven't got any of those fancy boxes.'

He reached into the back and started to grope about.
'If you'll let me pay for them,' I said.

'These are free range. I get twenty per cent more for
them at that Taybridge health food place than the
factory farmers get at the chain stores. But the wife
doesn't know, so don't tell her. They're her hens. Here.'

He held out the bag.

'Not unless I can pay.'

'Then I'll just have to drop them in the road, won't I?
You'll take these and you'll take my bitch, too. No charge
for either. I'll give you a ring.'

He slammed into what must have been the third of his
ten gears and the Land-Rover jumped into action,
leaving me by the side of the road holding a brown paper
bag already showing the leak signs from at least one
broken egg.

I was in the drive to 'Morvern', hidden by trees flanking
it, when I heard a car coming along the loch shore. I
turned my head in time to see a pickup truck flash past
the gates, Jock now driving at his usual speed. I wondered
where he had been in the last half-hour. There isn't
another house along the road south beyond 'Morvern',
just a telephone-box at a crossroads, and since there is
another one in the village I couldn't see him having to
drive a mile and a half if his own instrument was out of
order. And he hadn't been towing anything, so it wasn't a
breakdown. One of the little mysteries of country living
which happen daily.

Twenty minutes later it was solved. I was at the sink
draining-board doing my part in keeping up the local
tradition of opening tinned meat for lunch when I looked
up to see Aline coming across the courtyard towards the
back door. Coming isn't quite the word for it, either,
slinking would be nearer. She was wearing something I
had never seen before, a fringed Paisley shawl. This was
up over her head, covering her hair, and held under the

chin by one hand, a cowl that made her pale face
somehow suggest a refugee in flight from terrors behind
her. And she did look back once, then to right and left,
though never towards the house. I stepped back so that
she wouldn't see me if she did, watching her move faster
than I had ever seen her do before. I stood still, listening.

She opened the back door very carefully, not even a
creak of hinges in a house where these always need oil.
After that there was silence while she checked up on any
noises inside the house. I didn't think she would come into
the kitchen with her replacements for the contents of that
cigar box I had put in the stove, and in a moment or two
the treads on the stair cracked under her weight.

I thought about a confrontation, about following the
girl up to her room after giving her enough time to get the
syringe out and fill it, but decided against this. To tell the
truth, I was uneasy about doing that, not sure what could
happen with an addict in desperate need of her drugs. I
had seen in Aline the edges of what could develop into a
wild anger. The wise thing was to wait until she had
sedated herself and this time she might be careless about
where she hid the heroin, believing that I couldn't know
she had got fresh supplies.

CHAPTER 7

Aline came down very late for the cold lunch I had laid
out for her on the kitchen table. We didn't meet. This
was deliberate planning on my part. I prepared a trolley
for my tea-party and wheeled it along to the drawing-
room, then went to my desk to pretend to do accounts,
but actually to sit wondering what on earth had made me
buy a packet of baby food. The sudden impulse could be
interpreted as some kind of commitment to the girl and

her infant, and I wasn't having any of that. They were lodgers, no more, and of less importance to me, because of less economic value, than the family party of four from Leeds who had booked two rooms for a week at the end of June.

When I did go back into the kitchen it was to find from the remains that Aline had made quite a good meal before going back to her room, taking my portable radio with her. I could hear faint sounds of pop coming from it. Since there was no heating up there she was probably in bed, possibly feeding her son. The Bayola could stay at the back of my store cupboard. Running a guest-house means that you find a use for everything in time.

Geoffrey arrived at twenty past three, laden like a grocer's boy, and beaming. He had enjoyed his day. There were big changes in Taybridge, of course, but he felt that most of them were for the better. He liked the new chain stores which had successfully killed off nearly all the locally owned shops. You had to face up squarely, he said, to the facts of our time, and these included the non-viability of most small businesses. I nearly pointed out that another of the facts of our time, nuclear fission, isn't being faced up to all that squarely, but remembered that the good hostess's duty is to remain non-controversial.

I hadn't put on the drawing-room fire soon enough and the place wasn't very welcoming, flames sparkling away in the grate all right, but the area of heat penetration still minor, leaving most of the airspace still static at sub-arctic temperatures. Geoffrey held out his hands to the flames saying that it had turned quite bitter outside without adding that it was nice and cosy in here. We sat in chairs flanking the hearth and dug hard for old times.

He was much better at it than I was, telling me that I had once gone canoeing with him on the loch after midnight, about which I could recall absolutely nothing, the whole excursion seeming highly improbable, particularly since I simply couldn't imagine what we might have been up to *before* midnight. What I did remember was that in those days I hadn't found anything even remotely attractive about Geoffrey, my idea then being six-foot-three blond males of which Scotland has only a very limited supply and none of these ever came to Loch Riddoch in the summer.

About four I went along to the kitchen to brew up the tea and came back with the pot to find my guest standing at the table in the window with fingers of both hands lightly touching the Chinese bowl holding dried hydrangeas which so recently had also been holding something else as well. He turned his head.

'I hope you're careful with this, Sophia?'

I told him that I was moderately, that my mother had once had it valued and been informed it was worth thirty pounds, something she was fond of mentioning at tea-parties.

'A lot more than that these days would be my guess,' Geoffrey said. 'There's just the possibility it could be Tang. Though more likely it's a Ching dynasty copy.'

He was now facing me, expecting me to be surprised. I was, which gave him the perfect excuse for unveiling a facet of his personality which I might never have guessed was lurking there behind a façade of the safe and the respectable. He was a porcelain buff. Before he had told me much about this somehow improbable enthusiasm I began to get the feeling he had taken it up because it was something he could hide from his wife. This was exactly what he had done, starting by popping along to salerooms not five minutes from his Edinburgh office, at first only to look, then buying pieces now and again, never taking them home, keeping them at the office. He said Elspeth wouldn't have understood, adding with a smile of apology

to her memory that she would have thought it all a waste
of money.

It hadn't turned out to be that at all. He got quite good
at telling a Ching copy from the real Tang, or vice versa,
and the whole thing became as exciting as the gambling
casinos which are apparently the current kick for
Edinburgh's top people. It was no longer a matter of
cluttering his office with bits of bargain Imari, he began
to speculate, buying the doubtful in the hope that it
might turn out to be the authentic and making one or two
real kills which whetted his appetite for more. It was all
done with a certain cunning, too, which made it a lot
more interesting than roulette, pieces for which he felt
there was a real future in a rising market held for years at
the bottom of his Top Secret filing cabinet, but from
their dark hiding-places contriving to send out a glow of
warmth, like a laser beam, across a utility room to a man
sitting behind a standard issue executive desk.

I found myself positively fascinated at what I had
thought might turn out a near-ordeal tea-party. Geoffrey
complimented me on my connoisseur's tea, which I made
up of three parts cheapest Indian to one part cheapest
available Chinese, but he said nothing about the meat
paste sandwiches which weren't a success. At one point he
got up and walked around the room looking at Mother's
solid Victorian mahogany. His own taste in furniture was
Georgian, not that he owned any, Elspeth having
preferred 'modern'. He left me to guess at what that
might mean, and I could.

'Your Spanish mahogany is quite good of its kind,' he
told me. 'All this stuff is going to America. They just can't
get enough of it. Personally I'm not sorry to see it shipped
out.'

He looked around the room like an assessor.

'At least two thousand pounds' worth in here. Probably
a lot more.'

'*What?*'

I sat up straight. He had stopped at a davenport that was chipped and had lost a number of its knobs.

'You'd get at least eight hundred for this. It's a good specimen.'

I took a deep breath.

'What if that bowl in the window turns out to be Tang?'

'Oh, ten thousand at a sale in Scotland. Thirty thousand by the time it got to New York.'

'I see. And a Ching dynasty copy?'

'A couple of hundred. But it's a rising market. I'd hold.'

I don't know whether all this unnerved me, but over another cup of connoisseur's tea he suddenly started asking questions which didn't produce my usual defensive reaction to be being probed. He might have been the confidant I had been waiting for for years, and before I realized it we were off at a gallop. I think his asking permission to light his pipe, this granted, was a contributing factor in my coming to heel; he let out the fumes in little eruptive puffs that might have been American Indian smoke language. Also, we were surrounded by enough mahogany to have fitted out Freud's Vienna consulting-room, and he had what I can only call a brown voice which soon had the padlocks snapping on the door to what had hitherto been my carefully shut away private life. If I looked at the fire instead of Geoffrey it was a little like being seduced, and willingly.

'So you write, Sophia? Books?'

If he had said '*try* to write', I'd have clammed up.

'No. Just articles.'

'For what markets?'

I was warmed by the assumption I *had* markets. I looked at him instead of the fire and somehow wasn't disappointed.

'Well, just one really,' I admitted.

'What is it?'

I told him. The only publication which to date has seen fit to recognize my talents as a recorder of the passing show can't claim to have built up much of a reputation outside the area which it serves directly. In fact, if you asked ninety per cent of Scots what the *Perthshire Informer* was they'd probably suggest a new pensionable post established by the last Labour government. Actually it is a weekly newspaper published on Wednesdays which had just managed to hold on to its circulation of twenty-three thousand by totally ignoring the world outside our county, concentrating instead on detailed coverage of the annual general meeting of the Woman's Institute of Drumtoolie, this right down to the Chairperson's closing prayer at the end. My column, which is strictly rationed to three hundred and fifty words each week, appears as 'A Country Lady's Notes', a label which I have never felt fitted me too well, but was suggested by the editor so couldn't be queried. I am permitted on occasion to be gently satirical, but never for two weeks in succession, a tiny little bit of fun-poking in one issue must be followed in the next by one of my fairly lush nature notes extravaganzas. I have a completely mythical garden, this in no way resembling the horticultural austerity surrounding 'Morvern', in which I wander amongst bright herbaceous borders making suitable comments, all of which come straight from the head gardener of the parks in Taybridge. Fortunately for me, he is not the sort of man who would ever read anyone else's nature notes, even to sneer at them, and so far he has no idea that the woman who is always so interested in his flowers is none other than the 'Country Lady'.

No one else in Loch Riddoch or Taybridge has guessed either. Guarding the secret at the core of my life in a Highland valley has been one of the things that has kept me going. Whatever anyone in the area may think, I am not just a landlady, but have a hidden power they wot not of. Admittedly the power is held on a heavy leash by the editor, but there is always the possibility that a small snarl may just sneak past his proof-reading. Once or twice this has happened and there have been letters to the paper followed by a reproof over the telephone from the only man who knows who I really am.

That is, the only man before Geoffrey. To this porcelain collector and amateur psychiatrist I had suddenly revealed all and might have opened a door to disaster in my literary career. If the truth got out, nature notes or not, I would be shunned, facing a stony and highly unnatural silence in the post-office whenever I went into it and a head gardener running for cover when he saw me coming.

But Geoffrey was gentle in his triumph.

'I really am delighted, Sophia. It must be a *real* interest for you. And here I was wondering what on earth you found to do in the winter.'

'That's when I write most of my columns for next summer. You have to watch out what you say about the weather six months in advance, but there are no other serious risks.'

He beamed at me, suddenly looking rather like the Japanese god of good fortune in a scroll painting which Mother hung in the back passage in half dark because she thought the deity was showing rather too much tummy.

'Do you write for other markets as well?' Geoffrey asked. 'Or isn't there time?'

'There's plenty of time. But no other markets. I've even tried as far afield as New Zealand but not a single cheque has come through the post from a delighted editor.'

'Of course you'll be paid for your work on the—ah—*Perthshire Gazette*?'

'*Informer*,' I corrected. 'Yes, I'm paid.'

He had already got too much out of me. He wasn't going to uncover my real literary worth, which was a fortnightly postal order for six pounds. Last winter, in view of inflation, I suggested that they might put me up to eight pounds, which would have been four a week, a farm worker's wage in 1935 if you included free oatmeal, but the editorial reaction to this had been unfavourable. It was pointed out that most of the paper's correspondents didn't get a fee at all, just the honour and pleasure of seeing their words in print. I didn't press my case.

Geoffrey's departure left me with the feeling that I had behaved in a way completely outside my image of myself, something always so unnerving. He took with him my bowl which might be Tang, or Ching, or possibly contemporary Hong Kong, saying that he wanted a porcelain expert in Edinburgh to see it, and that he had to be in the big city next day to start in motion the clear-out of his house there. I suggested that this had to be the end of his economy weekend, rather hoping for ships that pass in the night and never send each other another signal, but that was not to be at all, the spell of Loch Riddoch had caught him again, and he had booked in for a month. He was only to be away one night.

As I closed the inner door after waving him goodbye the phone rang. It was from a call-box, the pips going madly even after I had shouted my name and number. Then there was a voice I recognized: Aline's boy-friend.

'Who the hell is that? I only got a little time on this line, see?'

'I've just told you! Miss McLinn!'

'Oh. Sorry. Look, I'm in one helluva mess. I don't know why I ever came to this goddam country. I swear I don't.'

'This is not making much sense,' I shouted.

'Sorry again. It's just that . . . they got me under arrest or something. I was tricked off the rig.'

'You were *what*?'

'Well, they said I was wanted in the Aberdeen office. I think maybe I'm getting another job. Could be back in Texas. So I just get in the helicopter. When I get out there's the cops waiting.'

'Where are you now?'

'Right at the airport. But it looks like they're taking me to Taybridge. The cops are from there. I got that out of them. They say all they want is a few questions. So why have to take me back to Taybridge? Being as polite as hell. I don't like it. Letting me phone but watching from their Ford to see I don't try anything.'

'Questions about what?'

'That guy Murdo. They say he's dead. I didn't know. How the hell could I? But they think I did know. I can see that. Look, I told them I was out on the rig when they found the body. It seems that don't make no difference. Because he was killed weeks ago. Because maybe I killed him then!'

There was an odd constriction across my chest.

'Nonsense!' I said. 'You're imagining that! They're questioning everyone who knew Murdo. I was, here in my own kitchen. And so was Aline.'

'The cops have been at *her*?'

'She knew him. Very well from what you've told me.'

'Oh God! I've got to talk to her. And she's got to help me now! I got no one else here. Call her, please! Those cops won't let me stay in here much longer. They're all staring at me right now.'

I didn't have to call Aline. She was on the front stairs, coming down them slowly, her hand on the banister. She might have heard Dean's shouting. She didn't ask if she was wanted.

I left the phone to her and went into the drawing-room, taking the poker to rake the remaining coals to one side for use in the cooker tomorrow. This room, minus the bowl in the window, could now be allowed to lapse back into its winter torpor. I wondered when I was going to be able to slump back into mine.

I could hear the mumble of Aline's voice, a word now and then, though he was still doing most of the talking. Or most of the shouting. I kept hearing bits of that shouting in my mind. 'She's got to help me! I got no one else!'

The girl's mumblings stopped. I put down the poker and set up the firescreen before crossing the room. She wasn't in the hall. The phone was back in its cradle. I went along to the kitchen. She was by the cooker, standing with her back to it, almost as though to face me when I came in. I closed the door.

'They'll be bringing him to Taybridge,' I said. 'To the police station. Are you going to him?'

She shook her head.

'How can I?'

'He wants you. He's asking for you.'

'I'm not going.'

'I'll look after the baby.'

'*You?*'

'Certainly! I'll let you have my car.'

'Thanks a lot. I can't drive.'

'Then I'll drive you.'

'Didn't you hear me? I said I'm not going. All this is not my business!'

'What *is* your business?'

'You've no right to ask that! Or to tell me to do things!'

I left her and went back to the phone. I can never remember my lawyer's number, always having to look it up. My glasses were in the kitchen and I took a long time peering at the book, holding it feet from me. I wasn't sure I had got the right digits but his wife answered. She was polite about my calling her husband at home instead of the office, saying that he was just putting his car in the garage, and if I could wait a minute she would call him.

It was a good three minutes before he came to the phone, minutes I was going to have to pay for. He was as polite as his wife had been. I had a perfectly simple question to ask, but my words suddenly seemed to wobble around it. He helped, not exactly patronizing, just the clear, professional mind offering assistance to a floundering, limited intelligence.

'What I really want to know is how long the police can hold a man?'

'Is he under arrest, Miss McLinn?'

'I'm not sure. I don't think so. But apparently they want him back in Taybridge for questioning. Supposing they have arrested him, how long could he be held before he was charged? Or whatever it is?'

'Overnight,' he said crisply.

'Is that *all*?'

'Yes. The police in Scotland do not have unlimited powers of detention, thank God. I hope I'm not alive to see the day when they do.'

'But what *happens*? Are you saying that the police have to decide before morning whether or not they are going to hold someone on a charge?'

'The police don't do the deciding. That's a matter for the local Sheriff after he has been in consultation with the Procurator-Fiscal. Miss McLinn, you haven't mentioned this American's name or given me any real indication as to how you are concerned in this matter?'

'I'm concerned in it because the police were here this morning asking me questions in my own kitchen.'

'Why didn't you get in touch with me at once?'

'Probably because there was too much to do.'

His voice went quiet.

'I want to know why the police were in your house asking you questions.'

So I told him. It was a relief, in a way, to do it. I was brief and he didn't interrupt with a single question.

When I had finished he told me that he was quite sure the police wouldn't bother me again provided I steered clear of the whole business, had nothing to do with the American again, and at once sent the girl back to the hotel chalets where she had come from.

'I can't do that at the moment,' I said.

His voice became louder.

'Miss McLinn, you can't, of course, know how serious this matter has become. I heard today at lunch-time. Unofficially. In spite of the body having been immersed in loch water and dragged about by currents for up to three weeks, forensic experts in Perth have been able to state positively that a bullet entered the dead man's forehead and emerged from the back of his skull, undoubtedly the cause of death. It is very unlikely that the wound could have been self-inflicted. The man did not drown. He was dead before he went into the water. There is some evidence to suggest that he was shot at some distance from the water and dragged to the point at which he could be pushed in. It would appear, therefore, that this is a case of murder.'

There is a chair beside the phone table. I sat down on it. It was a moment before I lifted the receiver to my ear again.

'Are you all right, Miss McLinn?'

'Oh yes. I suppose it was a bit of a shock. Well, surprise. Murder in Loch Riddoch. I don't think there's ever been one.'

'Yes, there was. In my father's time. A gamekeeper took an axe to his wife. He was hanged.'

There was a pause, then he said: 'I hope you see the position clearly now? You're to steer clear of this whole thing. This American could still be a suspect even if the police release him. The best place for him is back in those hotel chalets. And that girl with him. Under no circumstances allow the young man into your house. I don't want to sound harsh, but it is my duty to protect your interests. Wash your hands of this whole thing. And as quickly as possible. Is that understood?'

'Yes.'

'If that girl gives you any trouble about leaving, call me. I'll come out there and deal with her. And until you have your house to yourself again, and are completely clear of this matter, I want to know every move you make. Ring me here, or at the office. Any time.'

He hung up. I didn't at once get up from the chair. It had grown dark in the hall, suddenly night. A false spring hadn't yet been able to do much about lengthening our days towards the summer solstice. I got up. It's not often that I feel my age, an ache in the bones, but it sometimes happens. It goes away if you ignore it. It didn't go away as I walked to the kitchen door.

Aline was still standing almost exactly as I had left her, in front of the cooker, her hands held together at waist level. She might almost have been a wax model waiting for me to move her to a new position. It would be a charity to say that these rigid silences were a by-product of the drug, but I knew they were more than that, something she achieved by what had to be a positive effort of will, an anaesthetic against the life in which she found herself stronger than the heroin she also used.

'Get the baby ready,' I said. 'We're going to Taybridge to see Dean.'

CHAPTER 8

There had been hard frost after rain and I had to watch out for black ice, the car dancing on patches of it. Pete, wrapped in a quilt on the back seat, had no comment to make on our journey, as silent now as he had been when I carried him out to the Austin. Sometimes, when the glow from our headlights was bounced back into the car from trees, I could see in the mirror a movement of the quilt. He wasn't trying to kick himself free, just engaged in an experiment to see whether all his parts were working as they ought to be.

His mother, in the seat beside me, didn't move at all. Since Loch Riddoch she hadn't said a word. She was facing a cold night in almost the same clothes she had been wearing when I shut the door in her face, trailing skirt, a man's jacket, the ridiculous knitted scarf, everything except the hat. I hadn't seen the hat since it had been taken up to her room. Maybe she kept it for the really big upheavals in her life, the moves from one environment to another during which she needed its shade in which to shelter, though if this girl experienced fears at all I couldn't see her contending with them as the rest of us have to; instead she would wipe them away by reaching for a syringe.

Our road didn't just follow the windings of the Tala river down a valley but added an assortment of its own twists. In the Scottish Highlands the roads don't challenge the obstacles they meet, instead they wriggle round them, and often, when there is no need to, they go on wriggling, adding another bend every hundred yards simply from habit.

It was a shock to realize suddenly that Aline was crying. I hadn't really heard anything, there were no sobs, but when I looked at her I saw a shaking of her body that wasn't from cold, the heater was blasting out. She had her hands pushed down into her lap as though trying to control trembling by pressing clenched fingers hard between her thighs. There was a certain parallel between this situation and the ones I used to face in the Army with my girls, only then the hysterias had usually been noisy, with their origins obvious enough: an air raid, or a man, and even sometimes simple homesickness. There had been no issue manual on how to deal with these conditions, only an accepted approach; as a leader you offered firm sensible advice which usually worked, probably because it came from authority.

I couldn't see Aline accepting any authority. It would be my guess that her parents had never tried to assert it, allowing her self-expression amounting to being permitted to run wild. There are worse things than being brought up in a nursery with a gorgon Nannie who teaches little children that the Devil is out to get them if they don't watch out. The watching out is, after all, a kind of discipline. It helps to harden you up, like cold baths.

I let Aline shake, there didn't seem anything else to do. I didn't keep looking at her. It was a surprise when she said suddenly: 'I'm not going in.'

I still didn't turn my head, the road wouldn't allow inattention.

'I take it you mean at the police station?'

'Yes.'

'Even if he asks for you?'

'Yes.'

'You don't feel that you owe that boy anything?'

'Not really.'

'How long have you lived with him?'

It was some time before she answered, as though she had to work it out.

'About ten months.'

'What you've given him in that time balances out what he's given you?'

'Yes.'

She didn't have to think that out.

Angry, I said: 'Nice to be so sure.'

'I didn't want to be taken.'

I wasn't certain what she meant by that. Taken away?

If I asked from what I probably wouldn't get a sensible answer. I had harsh feelings towards her from the chemistry between us, which I couldn't see changing, and which therefore gave me no right to pass judgements even though I knew I would go on doing that. Towards this girl I had no duty at all and my lawyer was right, I wasn't to allow myself to have any. She was an accident to be dealt with by a certain competence, that was all.

'If you'd like a cigarette,' I said, 'there are some in the compartment in front of you.'

'I thought you never smoked?'

'I do it about three times a year. They're probably stale.'

The Austin had a lighter. She lit two cigarettes and passed one to me, which was a surprise. I sucked smoke into my lungs and coughed. It was incredible to think that I'd practically lived on the things once. PLC as I've heard it called, pre-lung cancer, only it wasn't fear that had made me stop, it was cost.

Aline didn't cough. The lights of Taybridge came up ahead. The town was settled into its winter night life, only three people on the pavements, everyone else watching television. If there was a scheduled choir practice in the lit-up church a lot would be missing it on the grounds of a wet night even though it had stopped raining. Near the centre were bright display windows but no one looking in at them. It wasn't a night for Bingo at the converted picture house, a frontage that had once glittered out all the delights of Hollywood, now sombre and with black graffiti on its side walls. A couple of pubs looked busy and the police station glowed a welcome.

I got out of the car without raising the matter of Aline coming in. Short of my carrying her, as I had her baby, there was no way to move her. I went up two steps into a tiled foyer to find a young policeman on duty with a mug of tea on the counter in front of him. It was an off night for crime in Taybridge, or maybe that started up much later.

'What can I do for you, Mother?' he asked.

I didn't care for that.

'My name is Miss Sophia McLinn.'

'Okay. What's it you want?'

It didn't seem to me that I was being offered the traditional politeness the police forces claim is being re-stressed these days, though maybe the new directives haven't had time to reach as far north as this.

'I believe you have a young man here under questioning? An American?'

'If you believe that you'll believe anything.'

'What do you mean?'

'There's naebody under questioning here. American or Chinee.'

It was a couple of minutes before I was quite convinced that the constable was telling me the truth, not just covering up for his superiors. The wound-up spring of my purpose in coming here seemed to snap, leaving me feeling rather a fool. I thanked the constable, which seemed to surprise him, then went out again into the lit paved area with which our local police advertise service at all hours.

It was snowing. Snow seemed to be a recurring theme to the background of my relations with the girl sitting in the car, only this time it wasn't just a feeble flurry, but serious, a layer of it already on the Austin's roof and settling on the windscreen, only melting on the still warm engine hood. I stood on a step and thought about the road back to Loch Riddoch. About half way there is a steep-sided, treeless glen in which snow always builds up, becoming a cork in the bottle of our valley. I wasn't worried about getting back to 'Morvern', there was still plenty of time to make home safely enough; the problem would be returning to Taybridge in the morning if by that time the police had brought Dean to their station in the town. We could be sealed away in Loch Riddoch for days, snowploughs still come to us last in spite of hopes that when the hotel-chalet complex was opened winter access to us would be improved for the tourist trade.

I went back to the car and got in.

'They haven't brought him here,' I said.

She didn't say anything. She had helped herself to another of my stale cigarettes and the car reeked of smoke. For the baby's sake there had to be some ventilation. I lowered the driver's window, switched on the engine, then reversed out of parking into the High Street. Her face registered no surprise when I braked in front of the Bellevue Hotel.

The establishment stays open in the winter, just. When my mother was alive and still mobile we sometimes lunched there, three courses, all highly reminiscent of the cuisine at the old Loch Riddoch hotel before progress took over. The Bellevue has been updated too, but only somewhat, still with plenty of mahogany around, and green tiles, and noisy plumbing. At one time it had two Automobile Association stars, but lost both, and now doesn't even claim a Recommend.

There was no one at reception. I rang a bell and stood there with a growing feeling that there was no one in the whole building. Then I was surprised by a voice from a dark passage.

'Yes? What can ai do for you?'

The hotel had changed hands, the present owners rumoured to be refugees from the south of England. The lady emerging into economy lighting was about my age, but made up for thirty years ago. She seemed to be wearing voile, all floaty side panels, with a head band around bright orange hair. It surprised her that I wanted *two* bedrooms.

'For one naight or more?'

'One night,' I said.

'Are you just passing through?'

'No. I live in the area.'

'Really?' There was a pause. 'Ai wish ai didn't.'

At once she tried to cover that.

'Would you be wanting dinner? The daining-room is open until naine o'clock.'

It didn't look as though anything was open. I asked to use the phone. She switched on lights in the cocktail bar and pointed to an instrument on the counter. Before renovation this place, labelled 'Lounge', had certainly looked like a dentist's waiting-room, but the conversion job to a corner of an old English pub wasn't my idea of a success, though they had tried hard, with a low false ceiling, plastic oak timbering and horse brasses.

My lawyer's wife was understanding about my need to speak to her husband out of office hours but when Mr Mackenzie finally came to the phone he wasn't so pleasant, listening at first with disgruntled grunts, then intense interjections leading to a final explosion.

'Have you taken leave of your senses? You've been pestering the police here about this American? What did you mean to do if you got in to see him?'

'Take him back to Loch Riddoch.'

He sucked in his breath for a shout. I held the receiver at some distance from my ear.

'You don't listen to me, do you? What's the point of having a legal adviser if you pay not one damn bit of attention to what he tells you?'

I was tempted to say no point at all, but was wise enough to allow him to empty out his feelings, the process going on for some time. Then, somewhat calmer, he told me what it did to his ulcer when clients behaved the way I was doing, thereby vastly complicating things both for themselves and for him. I said 'Yes, Mr Mackenzie' a few times until he was finally able to switch to the much

quieter voice he usually keeps for the matter of tax
avoidance.

'Well, what would you like me to do, Miss McLinn?'

I at least had an answer for that.

'Come with me tomorrow morning to help get the boy
away from the police.'

He returned to shouting.

'Why do you refer to this American as a "boy"?'

'Because that's what he is still.'

'Oh my God!'

Mr Mackenzie hadn't hung up, he was just breathing.
In the background I heard his wife protesting about the
kind of language he had been using over the phone. Our
local exchange is not yet fully automatic and ears still
listen on lines that are not theirs.

'I'm coming to see you,' Mackenzie announced. 'You
said you're at the Bellevue?'

'Yes.'

'Half an hour.'

He meant to see what was left of the television
programme I had interrupted.

The Bellevue bedrooms would be unlikely to tempt
anyone to stay more than one night even in high summer.
In winter they held a dank chill which a gas fire couldn't
begin to dispel. Through a connecting door I found Aline
already crouched over hers, with Pete on the hearthrug
still wrapped in the eiderdown. Somewhere in the lining
of that tweed jacket she had found a coin with which to
feed the meter. She greeted me.

'Could we have a coffee or something?'

'There's whisky coming up.'

'Oh. Having a night of it?'

I stood there wondering if anyone had ever hit this girl,
and if not why not?

'I'm hungry,' she told me. 'How about some
sandwiches?'

'I'll tell the proprietress when she comes up.'

'You know what that painted mummy said to me on the stairs? They don't take babies in summer. I thought for a minute she was going to ask about Pete's father.'

'Give me credit for my restraint,' I said. '*I* haven't asked you that.'

She looked up. The smile which never really quite arrived was being hinted at.

'Why not?'

'Possibly I thought it might embarrass you.'

'Hell!'

'Since it doesn't, who was Pete's father?'

'I don't know.'

'Your life was complicated at that time?'

'Not really. Not then. I never met him.'

She was looking at the gas fire again.

'That doesn't make sense.'

'Why not? Never heard of frozen bull semen being shipped out to the Argentine? I don't know whether the semen that helped make Pete was frozen or not. But it worked first time. The girl I was living with had to go back for repeats.'

I stood there, a survivor from a lost age, from a time when babies born out of wedlock were called love-children. There was a knock on the door of my room. I walked slowly away, my heart audible, as though it had been turned up to full power to get blood down into my calves and ankles.

The proprietress was standing on worn red carpeting with a tray on which was a bottle of whisky, a jug of water and, as though for an orgy, six tumblers. Perhaps she expected to be invited to join us, and she might have a husband kept in a cellar somewhere. I raised the matter of sandwiches and this seemed to please her, something else to put on the bill in the morning, along with the drink, and room service, and telephone. I was offered egg

and tomato, roast beef or, if I fancied it, pâté de maison
on fresh toast. This would be no trouble at all, the
Bellevue, along with all those Hiltons, offering snacks
throughout the night.

I took hold of the tray which wasn't at once
surrendered. We stood there united by its load, almost an
urgency on us both to remain in contact. What I needed
was to re-establish a norm for myself by the trivia of small
talk, at which I am so bad. I don't know what made the
proprietress hang on unless she was hoping for that
invitation, but perhaps all she had left on her TV set was
one of those celebrity games supported on hired laughter.
Across that tray we talked about the weather, specifically
the winter weather in the Highlands, this started by the
news that it was now snowing really heavily outside. She
hated being cut off among these mountains by bad roads,
adding something strange, saying that she had the feeling
a new ice age was coming, and that it would catch her up
here, the great white moving cliff coming so swiftly down
our valley that there would be no running from it to the
south.

She let go of the tray, putting up one hand to push
back tinted hair.

'Well, beef sandwiches it is. I'll send the gentleman up
when he comes.'

I took a double tot of whisky through to the girl, who
didn't thank me. She was exhibiting the kind of
peevishness that was usually totally wordless. It didn't
come from any expression on her face, more a kind of
emanation, like a sour smell of thought, a clear indication
that she was needing the syringe again. I was sure she
hadn't risked bringing it with her in that tasselled
shoulder-bag, not expecting to be parted from its support
for any length of time. I was feeling a kind of guilt at not
having challenged her over the replenishment of her
supplies, the plain fact being that I didn't want Aline in

my house suffering from withdrawal symptoms that I suspected might get violent.

I was having a whisky myself when Mackenzie knocked on the door. His eyes noted that drink was my secret vice, something that hadn't been brought to his attention before, and I think he was expecting me to sway en route to close the door to Aline's room. I came back to face him in front of a gas fire making popping noises.

'Thank you for coming at this time,' I said.

'That's all right. I've been on to the police. They're bringing the young man to Taybridge after all.'

'You mean they didn't intend to?'

'They haven't arrested him,' Mackenzie said. 'Just asked for his cooperation. The kind of request you can't really refuse, when it's from the police. Apparently the idea was to get him off the rig for questioning in Aberdeen. Then let him go back again if the answers were satisfactory. That was before our local police sergeant arrived on the scene with some new facts.'

'What are they?'

'I've only been told one of them. Your American "boy" had a gun. It wasn't licensed. It wasn't in his kit on the rig, he wasn't carrying it when he arrived in Aberdeen and there is no trace of it among his things in the chalet. They apparently have two witnesses to the existence of that gun, one of them a hotel maid.'

I could guess who the other was. I saw Aline sitting at my kitchen table, facing a police questioning.

'The gun was almost certainly a Colt .45,' Mackenzie told me.

It was a moment before I said, 'He may have taken it back to America. He was there for his father's funeral.'

'Left it at home, you mean? For safe keeping? Having discovered that our laws don't allow you to carry around unlicensed guns?'

'Well, why not? Or he could have thrown it away when

he discovered how things are over here.'

Mackenzie was staring at me.

'You seem determined to defend this young man. How often have you met?'

'Twice.'

'I see. You apparently assess character at some speed, Miss McLinn. Perhaps I should point out that a Colt .45 is not the kind of personal weapon it is easy to carry about in the inside wallet pocket of a jacket.'

It was improbable that Mackenzie had ever seen a Colt .45.

'I had as active a war service as women were allowed,' I told him.

'Ah yes, of course. Training to make snap judgements and stick by them, perhaps? Which is why you are now so certain that a man you've met only twice couldn't have used his gun offensively? To settle a private quarrel? About a girl?'

I had been waiting for him to bring Aline into it. I had no comment.

After waiting a moment for it Mackenzie said: 'Intuition is not something on which we can place much reliance in my profession.'

I had nothing to say to that, either. I offered him a drink. He declined, without adding that a lawyer never drinks on duty. Obviously an office pacer, he began to walk up and down. There wasn't much room for this with the twin beds and I had to stand nearer the gas fire with a glass in my hand and legs getting scorched. I sipped, glad of the whisky at this hour. He suddenly stopped in front of me.

'Miss McLinn, is it your impression that the young woman next door is devoted to her American lover?'

'No.'

'Then why do you think she stays with him?'

'There was no interesting alternative, until recently.'

'By alternative you mean the dead man? Murdo Menzies?'

'Yes.'

'In your opinion is the American devoted to the girl?'

'I think he has been. But if he isn't questioning those feelings now he ought to be.'

'In your view he would still be devoted to her at the time this Menzies was shot?'

'How can I answer that?'

'I asked it, Miss McLinn, because of your apparent total dedication to the idea that this American could in no way be involved in the killing of Menzies.'

'Total dedication is putting it a bit strong.'

'But you like him and you don't like her?'

'Agreed.'

'Your feelings about the girl are also intuitive.'

'No. Experience. She is far from an ideal guest.'

'Then why let her stay? Because her young man begged you to?'

I smiled at Mackenzie.

'I find I've become quite fond of the baby.'

Even a lawyer can show surprise. He was doing it. I could see him admonishing himself, always the learner, now revising an earlier assessment of my emotional potential before tucking this new evaluation away for future reference. I asked him if he would like to see the girl now and he said he would. I wondered what he was going to say to her.

'Quite simple, Miss McLinn. I'll point out that with developments in Loch Riddoch it would be wisest if she returned to that chalet in the hotel complex.'

'Supposing she's not in the least interested in doing the wisest thing?'

'Then I'll make it an order. With the suggestion that as your legal representative I can see that the order is enforced. By the police, if necessary.'

'Supposing I countermanded your order?'

He stared at me again for a good half-minute. His voice went gentle.

'In that case you would have to find yourself a new solicitor. There are two others here in Taybridge, but I doubt that you would be warmly welcomed by either. Perth is a long way to go for advice. Especially in winter.'

I opened the door to the other bedroom for him. Aline was feeding Pete in front of the fire, with the quilt from the car dangerously near to hissing blue flames. The baby was taking nourishment from her right breast, but both of them were exposed, the front of the grey dress under the tweed jacket comfortably unbuttoned almost to her waist.

'Aline, my solicitor wants a few words with you.'

She had been looking towards the fire. Her head came up and turned, transferring a stare. At my side Mackenzie was also staring, his expression now altered from the resolute man of the law of only a moment ago. It was my impression that this was his first experience of delivering an ultimatum to a nursing mother. I went back into my bedroom, pulling the door shut behind me, leaving him to it.

CHAPTER 9

I was coming along from a bathroom when I heard voices on the Bellevue's grand staircase, a man's and the proprietress's. The voices were growing louder. I went to a banister and looked into the well, on to the top of two heads.

The man said: 'Thanks, but I'm not hungry. I don't want anything.'

'Coffee would be no trouble.'

'No, thanks. But I guess I'd like to be called kind of early. Maybe around seven?'

'Certainly.'

The man had paused, as though for a rest. He didn't lower a duffelbag from one shoulder or put down a portable typewriter, just stood there, the woman in voile looking at him with interest. I went back to my room, standing behind the door with a crack to look through. Behind me was a mumble of one voice, Mackenzie appealing to reason and getting no reaction. It didn't sound as though he was near to an ultimatum. I stood watching the backs of the man and his guide, noting where they went. When I heard the woman's footfalls creaking back along the landing I left cover and went to yet another room rented out in a winter desolate hotel.

The man hadn't locked his door. He turned from delving into the duffelbag.

'My God . . . !' he said.

'We came to meet you at the police station,' I told him. 'But you hadn't arrived.'

'*What?*' Dean's voice was hostile. 'I don't get this.'

'I brought Aline in to Taybridge. You wanted that.'

'Look . . . I've forgotten what your name is.'

'McLinn.'

'Okay, Miss McLinn. Aline don't want to help me. She said so. Just like that. Straight out. So what the hell? I mean, why bring her in here to see me?'

'Maybe she's had a change of heart,' I said. 'Under pressure.'

'Yeah? Who's going to pressure Aline to do anything?'

He took a deep breath, and his time over it, as though it was a luxury he hadn't been allowing himself recently.

'Hell, I'm tired. I can't think. I'm sorry, I guess you're trying to help. But maybe you'd just best go back where you came from. What are you doing in this hotel?'

'Staying the night. Were you planning on going to

Loch Riddoch tomorrow?'

He nodded.

'How?'

'In my Fiat.'

'I thought the police brought you back?'

'Nope. I'm still free to go where I like. So long as it's where they want. And what they want is me in the chalet where they can have one cop watching. There's a manpower shortage.'

'What was to stop you driving anywhere you liked from Aberdeen?'

'Just a police car that happened to be behind me. All the way. But it was lucky it was right there when I got stuck in a snowdrift. Mighty helpful about getting me out again. As though they really cared what happened to me. If I'd just let them tow me all the way it would have saved gas.'

He sat down on one of the beds.

'I been cold all day, you know that? You wouldn't think a guy in from working on the rigs could feel the cold all that much. But I did. Even in that heated police office, here in Taybridge. In my guts.'

He put a closed fist against the pit of his stomach, in a limited way a mime artist. The tow-coloured hair was hanging down over one eye. I held out my hand.

'Matches and a fifty p. piece.'

'What for?'

'Heat,' I said.

He fumbled in the pocket of his tight jeans, pushing out a leg to get down into it.

While I was still on my knees in front of the fire he said: 'I felt like one of those sheep up on the hills.'

'Why?'

'Herded by a dog. All the way back here. That car with a blue light on the roof. Though they didn't have it

flashing. So I wouldn't get nervous. Just VIP treatment.
Escort.'

This fire popped worse than the one in my room. I
straightened, my knees cracking. I was irritated that they
had.

'I'm getting you some whisky,' I said. 'There's a bottle
in my room.'

'Lady, I wouldn't have thought it of you!'

He wasn't smiling. I went out along the passage to meet
Mr Mackenzie emerging into the hall. He wasn't wearing
the expression of a man who has just concluded a matter
entirely to his satisfaction.

'Is she going to leave all right?' I asked.

He sighed, shook his head, was about to tell me
something, but thought better of it and said good-night
instead, following this with a statement that he would
ring me when he had any news. Apparently I was to be
left with the problem of Aline totally unsolved. It could
be that I was now without a legal representative in
Taybridge, or would be in the morning when he'd had
time to think things over.

The connecting door to Aline's room was closed and no
sound came from beyond it. I took the bottle and two
glasses, suddenly reminded of wartime days when we got
our monthly liquor ration from the Army stores and then
had to decide whether or not to have an immediate orgy
or do the sensible thing and ration it out in little dribs and
drops over thirty days. Strange as it might seem to me
now, I had almost never been sensible.

Dean was still sitting on the bed, hunched over, staring
at his feet. I went to the washbasin, measured out a triple,
added a thumb width of water, then did the same for
myself, taking the two glasses across the room. I
remembered this euphoric feeling too from lost days, a
crisis still continuing but all the built-up tension suddenly
dissolving, as though some kind of mental mechanism

demanded a releasing of the nerve chocks, with a near-idiot sense of wellbeing beginning to surge up through you even though there was still masonry crashing and heavy bangs near at hand. You had been given a personal 'all clear', knowing that this time it wasn't you.

This time it was Dean, sitting hunched on a bed. He thanked me for the glass, sipped, considered the result of that for a moment, then took a decent drink. He looked at me.

'I guess you got the right idea, Miss McLinn.'

'Sometimes I do.'

'You know, it's funny. I mean, looking at you. I had a schoolteacher like you once.'

'Thanks.'

'No! I liked her. What I mean is . . .'

'Don't waste energy. You're tired.'

'Sure. Where's Aline right now?'

'In her room here. With the baby.'

He had another drink, thinking about that.

'I got to wondering about that kid sometimes. What's for him, I mean.'

'Did you like Pete?'

'No, I guess not.'

He felt that needed a postscript.

'I was okay with him. I mean we got on, kind of. I played with him quite often, when I was around.'

'Did Aline play with him?'

'Not that I saw.'

'Do you know why she had the baby?'

'Sure. There was a thing about it. Her friend was having one. With no man around. A lib thing. Or if there's men around it's only at parties.'

'You met Aline at one of the parties?'

'That's dead right.'

The fire was hissing steadily, not a comforting sound, almost sinister, like a continuous undertone of strings in a gloomy, contemporary symphony. Dean finished his whisky and put the glass down carefully on the tiles of the hearth.

'I'm paid off,' he said. 'Been good to know you, mister, but we don't need you on the rigs off Galveston either.'

'This means you're right out of the company?'

'That's it. Right out. Get the police interested in you and it's the next man in the queue takes over. How do I look after Aline now? And Mom needs money, too. Christ, there's no rest, is there? That's what I was thinking all the way back here. Driving that Italian car through Scotch snow. With the cops behind me. No bloody rest.'

He wasn't going to find it in the years ahead, either. If it wasn't Aline it would be another. The fatal mark was on him, tears and he would crumple to a stronger will. And the Alines can cry easily. She'd even switched on in my company, not that it had done her any good, whatever the object might have been. I was tempted to ask this boy whether a heroin addict is particularly unforgettable in bed. The question sat harshly in my mind but the schoolteacher he had identified in me wouldn't let it out.

Dean stood up.

'Am I going to get clear of this mess?' he asked. 'I mean, over Murdo?'

'Yes.'

'How can you be so damn sure?'

'You didn't kill him.'

'You think I couldn't have done? I'll tell you something, I hated that guy. He was never around when I was back here, but plenty when I was on the rig. It leaked out in bar talk at the hotel. The kind that cuts out quick when you come in, which means a big arrow pointing straight at you. It was a sort of build up. For a long time I wouldn't look at what was happening. I didn't see it. Even when I knew for sure I didn't say anything to Aline. Not until that night she came to you. Then we blew up. What I called her and she called me. You know this, she came back stronger than I would ever have guessed she could. With a kind of hate in it. That's when I threw her out. And when she had gone I was sick. Now you know.'

I had known for some time. He was staring at me.

'You think Aline blabbed to the police?'

'I think she told them what they wanted,' I said. 'Probably with her usual economy. But all they needed.'

'Which means that right now the cops think I put that guy in the water. With a bullet.'

'They'll change their minds.'

'You can say that. Who the hell else would? Okay, so I'm clear. I beam back to the States. You can get work of some kind in Dallas, even these days. But it's Aline. How do I get her back home? On narcotics and that really showing?'

The simple answer to that was he shouldn't try to. I said nothing.

'She won't marry me,' Dean announced.

It was one of the few things I could put to her credit, though it was improbable there was any virtue in it. I picked up his glass and at the washstand did a repeat of the medicinal dosage. He took what I handed him and gazed at its colour.

'Finish that, Dean, then get some sleep. We'll go back to Loch Riddoch tomorrow. The police will let you?'

'Like I said, it's what they want. One cop watching.'

'We'll make it a little harder for them. You'll settle up with the hotel for the chalet, then move down to "Morvern".'

'*What*? Look, if you think I'm short of money or something . . .'

'It's not money, it's Aline. She may need looking after and I can't do it on my own.'

'Because she's on speed, you mean?'

'No. Because the police may well be back with more questions to put to her. And one of us ought to be there.'

'You haven't said what you think Aline told the cops. And you know, don't you?'

'Yes. There were two witnesses to the fact that you have a gun. Or did have one. The police know it was a Colt .45. From a pretty good description. They could have got that from Aline or the maid who cleaned the chalet.'

'I'm to take my pick?'

His voice was harsh.

'Dean, there's only one thing I want to know about that gun. Are the police likely to find it?'

'Not unless they bring a midget submarine to this goddamned lake.'

Someone had put out the light in my room and there was no glowing crack under the door to Aline's. I accepted that signal; it was what I wanted, too. I couldn't have borne to look at her right then.

We didn't have a police car tailing us to Loch Riddoch. There hadn't been a plough clearing the road but some kind of heavy duty vehicle had used it, the tracks plain enough, and on the high moor where the snow was worst I settled the Austin's tyres into those tracks, only skidding out of them on some of the bends. It was a glittering morning, the sun so strong off white that I nearly reached for my sunglasses. Dean followed in the Fiat.

We had breakfasted together in a chilly dining-room near another gas fire only half on, four of us including Pete who was propped up in a chair on cushions provided by the proprietress who now seemed quite taken by this guest she wouldn't have allowed under her roof in summer. Three of us had bacon and eggs, the man of the party with two eggs in the British tradition, when it was really me who needed them. The only one who had done any talking was Pete. He wasn't noisy about this, no yelling, just sat and chatted to no reaction. I thought I picked up quite a strong note of protest in that monologue, maybe he was wanting bacon and eggs like the rest of us.

En route to a final visit upstairs I rang the bell on the reception desk and the proprietress, converted back from being waitress and cook, came out of her office to tell me that the bill for the whole party had been paid, via cheque and banker's card, by the baby's daddy. I didn't protest about this to Dean, the responsible will always insist on assuming responsibility. It seemed likely that before he flew back to the States, with the threat of a murder charge removed, he would be considerably in my debt again.

Back in Loch Riddoch, we went first to the hotel complex to let Dean pay yet another bill, after which I followed the Fiat up to the chalet. Dean called out that he would be only ten minutes or so and I suggested to Aline that I could look after the baby if she wanted to help her lover pack. There was absolutely no reaction to this, not a word spoken, but I still got the message that what she didn't want now, or later, was to be alone with Dean. At breakfast, and after, both had been playing the children's game of refusing to look at each other, almost tempting me to offer a prize to the one who held out the longest.

It was all of twenty minutes and getting cold in the car before Dean emerged lugging a couple of huge suitcases, stowing these in the Fiat along with his duffelbag and typewriter. He then went back into the chalet, to come out carrying something wrapped in a cloth with what looked like a teddy-bear tucked under one arm. The teddy-bear was held out towards Aline in the Austin's back seat.

'I suppose you forgot this because I gave it to the kid?'

The girl had no comment. Dean handed me the thing wrapped in cloth. The covering fell away to reveal a four-inch-high silver cup with fancy handles and an engraved message.

'I won that in my Junior year at Wichita Falls High School,' he said. 'Swimming. My only damn prize. I carry it round to bring me luck. Think it's doing it?'

He grinned. I was glad to see that.

'Morvern' gave us one of its chilliest welcomes, the kitchen range not only out, but stone cold. Aline only stayed in the kitchen long enough to heat the water for a stone 'pig', then went upstairs to join the baby. I don't think Dean had ever before seen a coal-fired range, but the rig worker seemed interested in this relic from the pre-technological age, insisting on cleaning out the firebox, inspecting dampers and flue access hatches, finally carrying the ashes out to a dump beyond the fuel shed.

In a kind of embarrassment for my old stone house I bustled, getting out my stockpot, the like of which Dean hadn't seen before either.

'What's it made of? Lead?'

'Iron,' I said. 'In Scottish crofts there used to be one always on the simmer by the fire, night and day. You threw everything into it.'

'For soup?'

'No, stock.'

'It's one kind of cooking, I guess,' he said.

'I only use mine sometimes. And the rest of my pans are aluminium. In case you're worried.'

I think he was, a little. Then the fire started to crackle and give off heat, with Dean bent over it making percolator coffee. I peeled a turnip and scraped carrots.

The front doorbell rang. Dean straightened.

'I'll go,' I said, drying my hands.

The detective-sergeant was standing neatly on the mat, as though wherever possible he tried to do this to avoid marking up polished vestibule tiles.

'You're even quicker than I expected,' I said.

He didn't bother with a politeness.

'Where is he?'

'In my kitchen. Only there won't be any interrogation in there this morning. I'm cooking. You can use the sitting-room.'

'We can use the police station,' Dean said from behind me.

Without turning I said:

'No!'

Neither of the men seemed to have heard me. Though Dean didn't touch me I had the feeling of being pushed out of his way. I stood watching them go down the steps to crunch away over gravel towards the police car. Our village constable was standing by it. He gave me a nod which I didn't acknowledge. The Ford left my grounds at an important speed, taking the gate too fast. I half expected to hear the siren switched on, but it wasn't.

Back in the kitchen I washed the floor to the news from a set which Aline, on some whim, had returned. The condensation of world events didn't seem very important, even further removed from Loch Riddoch than usual. A weather forecast following could have been written by that prophet of doom from many centuries ago, the Braham Seer, the man who forced the Scots to invent whisky in order to be able to face the future only semi-conscious. We could expect sleet driven by Force Eight winds across deeply iced mountains. Those first snowdrops along my drive had all been eaten by starving sparrows.

All of an hour later, with Dean not back from the police station, and no sounds from above to suggest that Aline was hungry and coming down, I was sliding a casserole into a hot oven when the phone rang. I took so long to get down the hall I expected the caller to give up before I reached the instrument, but he hadn't. The man's voice seemed distorted by a bad line.

'Miss McLinn? Loch Riddoch?'

'Yes. Who's calling?'

If he gave a name I didn't hear it. I shouted that he was to speak up and he did that, but still wasn't very distinct.

'I'm afraid . . . an accident.'

'What kind of an accident?'

'Car. A Mr Connors. A Mr Geoffrey Connors. The car is a write-off.'

CHAPTER 10

I can't always count on my mind at once coming up with a respectable reaction to bad news. This time I didn't see poor Geoffrey lying bleeding by the side of a road, instead had a flash vision of that shiny new Metro reduced to a heap of scrap metal. My thought was . . . what a waste. After that I was able to ask the right questions and, to do myself justice, with increasing concern. The voice informed me that Geoffrey wasn't hurt except for a bit of bruising, but it appeared that he was in some kind of shock, absolutely refusing to leave his wrecked car. The voice hadn't known what to do about this, in fact there was nothing he could do except leave the accident victim.

'I tried my best to get him to come on with me to Perth. He wouldn't. I'm a commercial traveller. I've an appointment I can't miss, so I couldn't take the time to bring him back to Loch Riddoch to your garage. Now I'm really worried. I feel I haven't done all I could have. Especially since it looked like snowing again up there.'

'Up where?'

'The back road over the Ben Tala hump. I use it when I've been in Loch Riddoch. Even in winter when it's open. So much quicker than going round by Taybridge. Lucky

I was pushed for time and risked it today. I didn't meet another car all the way down here.'

'Where are you now?'

'Bengarnich village. On the other side of the mountain. It's the first phone-box I've come to.'

'Geoffrey asked you to call me? For me to get on to our garage?'

'Yes. Will you do that?'

'Of course. At once. Where was the accident?'

'Just beyond that old quarry below the pass. About ten miles from you.'

Twelve miles would be nearer it. It seemed that the Metro had skidded on a bend and dropped twenty feet on to rocks. Geoffrey was lucky on that road that it hadn't been a hundred feet. I could only see the idiocy of his risking the back way to Loch Riddoch on a winter's day, and after a snowfall, as part of the new life patterns into which he had hurled himself with such remarkable abandon. You recaptured youth by taking risks. If this incident hadn't put a check on the process he might well yet decide to become part of the back-up team for an ascent of Kanchenjunga in the Himalayas.

'How was the road surface up there?' I asked.

'Not bad at all. The wind has blown most of the snow off it. I only had trouble in one or two places. None at all coming down this side. But if it snows again it could be pretty awful.'

'Well, I'll get on to the garage at once. Then I'll come up myself.'

'No! He doesn't want that. He was specific that you're *not* to come.'

I wasn't to be allowed to see the new Geoffrey in a somewhat dishevelled state.

'I'm coming anyway,' I said. 'He'll need some hot soup.'

'In that case he's in a hut in the quarry itself. I helped break down the door. But don't be long in getting up there in case it snows again.'

'I won't be long.'

The voice hung up. I dialled the Loch Riddoch garage but there was no answer. Just in case I'd got the number wrong I dialled again and let the burring go on for a good two minutes. No one lifted the receiver at the other end.

If the Metro had dropped twenty feet off the Ben Tala hump road there was precious little that Jock's breakdown truck could do in this weather, or in any weather for that matter. It sounded as though the job was going to need a crane from Taybridge. I had no doubts about being able to persuade Geoffrey to abandon the wreck and return to Loch Riddoch with me; if he had been suffering from some form of shock hysteria a considerable spell of waiting in a freezing hut up in that quarry should have gone a long way towards curing him. I decided not to go on trying to contact the garage, and, since Jock was certain to charge some ridiculous hourly rate for doing nothing, this way I was saving a friend money, which is always a nice thing to do.

I got back to the kitchen to find Aline in occupation along with Pete, who was wrapped in a shawl, propped up in a chair and wide awake, but making no noise, a remarkable feature with him from the little I knew of babies. His eyes were on the alert, noting my return, and apparently approving of it, which, for no reason that made sense, I found rather pleasing. Aline was sitting in a straight-backed chair, the paper I had brought back from Taybridge flat on the table in front of her. Her sudden interest in world news could be that she was hunting for the latest on the Murdo Menzies story that had so far only been reported as a drowning.

I went about my business, warming up soup, my moving about continuing to be unacknowledged by my paid-for house guest, this leaving me untroubled. When I had filled the Thermos to be used in succouring Geoffrey

I went to stand in front of the girl. I used a stronger than conversational voice to get her attention.

'I'm going to have to be away for a time, maybe an hour and a half. There's a casserole in the oven. Tinned meat so it doesn't need a lot of cooking. In about twenty minutes I want it taken out of the hot oven and put in the slow oven underneath. Can you do that?'

She looked up and nodded. I took advantage of this to explain the situation in some detail, then added that if I wasn't back in a couple of hours it would probably mean that I was in some kind of trouble myself. Aline was then to ring the hotel to let them know that one of their guests, Geoffrey, had been in an accident up the back road over Ben Tala and would they send the hotel bus, which has snow tyres, up that road to fetch him. It was perhaps a shade pompous of me to add:

'Think you can handle all that?'

'I'm not a moron,' Aline said.

And on that note we parted. I took my Thermos of soup out to the Austin, which started at once without a sputter as though advertising the good old British reliability we used to believe in. The windscreen wipers worked, too, polishing frosted glass. I put the heater on full and sat there for a moment like a plane pilot for the warm-up before a tricky take-off, revving for a hint of cylinder knock that could mean trouble during what was going to be a long, low-gear climb. The fuel gauge said three gallons, a lot more than I ought to need. I had put in two before leaving Taybridge, using one of the new automatic pumps that don't sneer at you for buying your fuel on the instalment plan. It's years since I had a full tank.

The flat along the shore from the gates of 'Morvern' offered assorted tyre tracks in the snow but at a cross-roads most of these swung right when I had to go left, with only the record of one set of heavy duties for me to follow. These could have been left by the man who found Geoffrey, and I was certainly grateful to the trail breaker who must have a heavy car, for in places asphalt had been bared, giving me good traction just where I needed it most. It's not the kind of driving I enjoy, but the challenge was interesting none the less, demanding an almost aggressive approach. I had to go much faster than was good for the engine in low gear, and there were grumbles from it, but I was able to hold speed when a slackening could have meant a slither into a snow bank. In places the heavy duties that had gone before had skidded, peeling snow from the road surface, this often helping me around bad corners. It was encouraging to remember that the early bends on the hump road were the worst and the steepest, with after them much gentler gradients and looser turns, these leading up on to heather moors.

I got out of the birchwoods flanking the first two miles of the climb from the valley into the open where the light was a white shining off snow. A passenger would have seen wonderful views; I saw the road, pressing down and then easing the accelerator, keeping the engine whine steady, getting the Austin up to thirty miles an hour in places. I had one or two skids but none of them serious. The cloud bank which had seemed so threatening down in Loch Riddoch was much less so up here, still dark enough to hold a lot more snow, but moving east quite fast, with breaks in it that offered slits of pale yellow winter sunshine, like light shining through cracks in an old floor.

In spite of the light Ben Tala was in a grim mood. From the beetle of the Austin crawling up its flank there was an uninterrupted sweep to the summit, from here the volcanic cone shape more pronounced than in the valley, with its peak just failing to punch a hole through the cloud mass above it. Even in summer these high moors feel utterly lonely, the narrow road over them an irrelevance unlikely to lead anywhere, but under snow the scene becomes antarctic, a sense of desolation to the mountainous horizon and probably a hundred horizons beyond.

At this height there was a new hazard, icing in the tread marks left for me by the heavy duties. If I were to lose traction because of this the car would go into an uncontrollable slide. I pushed the engine to revs that had it screaming. The speedometer needle dropped back. The tyres sent out sprays of soft snow..

Then there was reprieve. The Austin pushed over a crest and was on the level, which lasted for long enough to let me get up speed for the next gradient which was much gentler, leading to what I remembered was an almost surprise drop into the ravine which held the quarry. On this sudden downslope I used the gears for braking but still went a lot faster than I liked, which was probably why, though I must have seen this, the fact that the tracks I was following turned into the quarry, leaving the road beyond untouched snow, simply didn't register.

I followed the tracks. The quarry floor was flat and I came to a careful halt about half way across it, switching off the engine. I then realized that the vehicle which had laid those guiding tracks for me was here, parked within yards of the Austin, a big, dark blue van. Along its side was white lettering 'Murchie of Perth', then underneath 'Rent-a-Van'.

It must have been a harassing drive that had sedated my mind. It certainly took me a long time to come to any conclusions about what I was looking at, that van and, straight ahead, the old workman's hut with a tin chimney coming out of the roof. Its door was shut, the one window had been boarded up. I wound down the glass beside me and sat listening. If there was a wind on the moors not a hint of it came into the quarry, the air still, the silence total. It seemed the sensible thing to get out of the car to find out why a rent-a-van had been driven up this winter isolated road to park in a quarry. At that point I had absolutely no sense of the highly unusual as any kind of threat to me. It was almost as though I had momentarily forgotten about Geoffrey and my reasons for coming up here.

I opened the door and used it to hold on to as I climbed out, my legs stiff from the muscular tensions of the drive, and I was still holding on to it when the hut door opened, quite slowly. There was someone standing there. It certainly wasn't Geoffrey, much too tall. He was dressed for skiing, dark trousers, heavy blue sweater, a black balaclava with an oval hole for the eyes pulled down over his face. He held a gun loosely at hip level. Even from that distance I recognized it, a war surplus 303. He raised it slowly.

Fear hit me like a blow on the back of the neck. It certainly concentrated my attention. The 303 has a muzzle mouth like an eye. I have drilled with it, the real gun, not a dummy. Once I fired five rounds from it on a range, no bull's eye, but four in the inner circle.

The man was certainly taking his time, no need for him to hurry, not up here. He might have been a sportsman offered a target it would be a disgrace to miss, half ashamed at having things made so easy for him. I stood there, still holding on to the car door, with the idiot question in my mind why he had chosen a 303. It's not an easy gun to carry around or for someone not in the Services to come by these days.

He wasn't used to it, either. To get me in the sights he had to put his head down at an awkward angle, chin lowered, like a violinist tucked into his fiddle. Then the rifle settled against his shoulder. I was rigid, fear washing out thought, except one half formed. I seemed to know why he didn't pull the trigger. You don't shoot a motionless quarry at close quarters. His disciplines forbade it. A decent kill means you wait for the frantic escape effort certain to follow your victim's seconds of frozen staring. You wait for a wild leap to get away. Then you fire.

I made a partial recovery from terror in those seconds. I could plan, resisting helplessness with a game. My one chance was that game against his disciplines. What I did must have looked convincing enough. It checked his cold purpose for the time I needed.

My faint was only half pretence, my knees were dissolving under me. My hands had gone slack on the steel framing of the car window. A bullet would punch through the metal of the door if he fired. He didn't. I heard my heart. It sounded like an overworked marine engine. It might have been pushing needed blood to my brain.

My body held the door open as I slid down it. I turned slightly to crumple on the ground, face down, my arms under me. At once the cold of snow came through my clothes. I mustn't shiver. There was no sound at all, except the thumping of my heart, like a clock ticking off seconds. Then the clock quietened. I was aware of the silence beyond me, all around in that well of the quarry.

There was a crunch on snow, then another. He was coming. I wanted to scream. I wanted to give up my pretence, to lift my head from snow wetting my hair to make a last protest. Not screaming was like trying to control nausea, keeping the vomit from rising.

I had to fight against trembling. I wanted to look, to see whether the gun was still tucked into his shoulder as he came towards me. He would notice if I moved my head. My game would end if he was carrying that gun high, ready to fire.

The crunch of his footfalls stayed slow, but getting louder. I thought I heard his breathing. I had wanted him as close as this, coming to believe that I really had fainted. I pushed up on my arms. I was on my feet and running almost in one movement. I ran towards the back of the blue van.

He may have fired from the hip. I heard the bullet, it hit rocks, ricocheted, then whined over the quarry. When he fired again I was around to the rear of the van. I ran up behind its shelter to the driver's door, wrenching this open. The key was in the ignition. I turned it before I was even in the seat. The engine rumbled. I kicked the clutch and pushed in a gear without seeing which one it was. The van jerked backwards. I think the man had to jump to get out of the way. He may have fallen. I couldn't see him in the mirror.

I slammed into a forward gear and at once the heavy vehicle began a slide over the soft snow on the quarry floor, out of control. I fought to get a tyre hold but the swinging about continued. Then suddenly the hooded man was standing directly ahead.

I revved the engine, trying to steer straight at him. He fired. The windscreen stayed clear. He fired again as the van swerved. The wheel shuddered under my hands, then went hard as the offside front tyre flattened. Snow sprayed out from under the fender.

The man had lowered his gun. He knew I wouldn't get far on that wheel rim; but I got further than at first seemed likely. The engine screamed. I might have been belabouring a lamed horse. Soft snow had kept the wheel from fracturing, but when this happened the whole of the van's forward weight would come down on the hub.

I got much further than I was expecting, at some speed and with a great deal of noise. Then there was a louder noise, a crack. The van tilted. Steering went rigid. If the man was coming after me I couldn't see him in the mirror. I was sure he wouldn't be hurrying, which gave me time. I didn't want to be caught in the cabin, to be ordered out of it. I had the feeling that if I heard him speak my will to resist might crumple. If I had to die I wanted it to be running, trying to do something. I was afraid that faced at close range with the blunt fact of death I might humiliate myself, even plead for life. I didn't want to go like that, in shame, making a nothing of every year spent behind me.

The list of the van put the driver's door high above ground, with the offside one half buried in snow. I had to jump. I straightened from doing that to look about. There was no sign of the man and no tracks to indicate that he had followed the van, now hiding behind it. I saw movement amongst a tumble of rocks at the quarry wall. He fired.

The bullet was meant to frighten me. It seemed to skid along the roof of the van, noisy, and far off target. Even with a heavy 303 to which he wasn't accustomed he wouldn't miss as wide as that. He wanted me to run. My game was now his game, being played by his rules. The hunter wanted a clean kill at a decent range, and the longer the range the more credit to him.

He wanted me to run. I did. There was nothing else I could do. Though it wasn't exactly running, more a floundering through snow which had drifted by the opening from the quarry to the road. I never considered trying to get back to the Austin, certain that if he saw me attempting that he would abandon his game and drop me before I could reach the car door.

I was going for the road. All the way up the slope I had brought the Austin down there was cover of a sort, a bank with irregular outcrops of rock. And there were those tyre tracks for my feet. I could run up them faster than he could make his way through snow. By the time I got on to the moor I might be well ahead of him, out of his range. And from there on my road home was down.

He let me out of the quarry, and out of his sight. I

couldn't really understand that. I didn't want to. I wanted to hope that my plan was stronger than his, and that when I got up this gradient I would almost be running free. The terror would still be behind me but diminishing on the downslope, with the prospect of cover ahead where the birchwoods started, these thin at first, but thickening, then finally giving way to the scented forest of pines. Under these was sanctuary in deep shadow.

I had forgotten one thing: the years behind me. I couldn't run up the tyre tracks, I hadn't the breath for it. I had to walk, and gasping. There was shock that I was reduced to this, that there wasn't a reserve to be called on. I had spent my reserve. My heart and my breathing told me that, and were loud about it.

The hunter knew me. He knew my age. He knew that running a boarding-house, even the going up and down stairs in it, doesn't keep you fit for hill walking. He had seen me using my Austin more and more and my bicycle almost never. I was still in his game, even on that road where I had cover all the way up to a little summit from which there was a view of Loch Riddoch if the mist hadn't come down. I was sure there would be no mist, that I would be granted that view. He would never have let me get as far from him as this if there had been any risk of fog closing in to blur his target for the serious shot.

I slipped on an icy patch and fell, flat on the road. I wasn't down for more than seconds, but the temptation to just stay there, waiting, was strong. I got up on all fours first, then pushed back on to knees before struggling to my feet. Before moving on again I became conscious of the white slope of Ben Tala sweeping up to my right, no summit visible, clouds covering it. Under snow the mountain was sinister. I remembered the woman in the hotel and her ice age coming.

Walking again I tried to make it half a run, but my

body was awkward and felt heavy, as though I was carrying a great deal more weight than I ever have in my life. There was no second wind coming to help me. I kept my head down, watching my feet. I didn't know I had reached a crest on the road, up on the moor, until I was clear of the bank's shelter and the light around me grew brighter. Then I looked up.

The tyre tracks now sloped away, down. Below was the world in which I had lived. The waters of Loch Riddoch were dark but the village beside it was illumined by snow and seemed to shine. I could see the humped bridge and then a plain, granite house half hidden by trees.

I turned my head to look back.

The hunter had got what he wanted, a long range for a difficult kill. He was up on a hummock of moor, silhouetted against the grey clouds that went on to shroud the top of Ben Tala. I could see that the gun was in his shoulder. I may have moved as he fired. I heard the bang. For a second I saw the white snow into which I was falling.

CHAPTER 11

There was a voice:

'If she comes round she's to get an injection. You give it. At once.'

Another voice:

'Yes, Sister.'

The second voice might have come from one of my girls up before me on a charge; a note of subservience that was false. I knew where I was. The injection would be to make me unconscious again. I didn't move, giving them no excuse to use the needle. I wouldn't let them make a dark for me, I make my own. The feeling was strong, set in a kind of stubbornness.

My hand was lifted. My body nearly stiffened. Then I knew it was my pulse being felt for. The hand was lowered again.

The Sister, condescending, said: 'Doctor's still afraid of pneumonia. I'm not. She's a tough old girl.'

Feet moved away, out of the room, the sound of them dying squeakily in a corridor. The girl who was left began to hum. I risked a look at her.

She was at the washbasin, turning on taps, the humming an imitation of chords struck on a guitar. She had her back to me. I had a look around without moving my head. I was in one of those separate cells which offer the National Health patient free privacy when death is imminent. My left arm seemed to be held rigid to receive the plasma drip. I didn't try to move it. I had never been inside the new Taybridge hospital but was reasonably certain that was where I now lay.

The girl at the washbasin was certainly strong, given to more vigorous movement than the job in hand really required, the kind of help I need at 'Morvern' and can never get. While I watched she wrung out the cloth she was using, hung it on a hook under the basin, washed her hands, then pushed her face close to the mirror, fingers prodding at what was probably a pimple.

For the first time I looked down at the arm they had taken over to pump plasma into me, not liking what I saw. I didn't need or want that alien blood. In spite of the private room I knew I was all right. Without really meaning to, I moved slightly. The pain was astonishing, a dagger stab from somewhere below my right shoulder and above my breast. I don't think I made a sound but the girl at the washbasin dropped her hands and spun around. I was sure I had shut my eyes in time, but there was still a good half-minute of tension in that side ward while she watched me. Then I heard something clink, and knew she was coming towards the bed.

If it was the needle I was going to fight that, pain or no pain. Then, from the way she lifted my hand, I was sure it was the pulse she wanted to check. If I lay still my heartbeat would quieten. She cheated me. I felt the prick of a needle. I tried to jerk my arm away. She was ready for that, a strong girl.

I must have done some intense dreaming. There is a half recollection of flying, cruising quite high above mountains, like a bird of prey looking for its victim. My view was of the kind that must make hang-gliding exciting, though I wasn't clinging on to anything, perfectly free, floating gently, peering down at those mountains which didn't look at all like Scottish mountains, much more jagged, volcanic, unsmoothed by an ice age.

It is odd to come back from being a golden eagle, or a condor, to find yourself looking at your lawyer. I didn't at once see him, first it was a square of window from which the light was too white, a glare, giving me a sense of midday or a little later. I also had, almost at once, a feeling of time lost, of not knowing what day I had come back into myself again. I turned my face away from the brightness.

Mr Mackenzie was sitting in a hospital chair set back against one wall. He didn't give the impression of a solicitor waiting patiently for a client's death, instead he seemed to be using the time in my private room to get on with business that might have been subject to telephone interruptions in his office. There was a black suitcase on his knees, a file open on top of it, a pencil in one hand and spectacles on his nose. That composed industry was reassuring, and it didn't occur to me then that the prospect of my demise wasn't likely to be something that would worry him too much. Instead, as I watched him make a note on the edge of the file, I had a surprising sense of his closeness to my living, this a bit odd in view of the fact that he was sitting just about as far from me as anyone could in that private cell. I had a sudden urge to communicate, and was perhaps a bit too ambitious in my choice of words.

'These days . . . they bring you back . . . when they want.'

What I wished to convey was that, just as they can knock you out by the prick of a needle, they can bring you back with another prick. I'm not sure that this is in fact the case, but it seemed brilliant at the time. Mr Mackenzie, however, wasn't particularly appreciative. He plucked off his glasses, looked at me solemnly for a moment, then said:

'Ah.'

'You,' I told him, 'are my first visitor.'

He nodded. 'I persuaded the police to let me be.'

There seemed something slightly sinister in that which had the effect of putting our relationship back into perspective. Perhaps as a result of this I felt considerably stronger.

'Have you been waiting long?' I asked politely.

'About half an hour.'

'You mean you've been sitting there on the off-chance I might wake up?'

'Not exactly that. The Matron phoned that you were expected to come out from sedation at any time.'

It was interesting that I was establishing myself as a model patient, coming around on schedule.

'How long have they kept me unconscious?'

'The better part of two days. It was thought wisest in the circumstances.'

'Meaning my age?'

'That was never stated, Miss McLinn.'

'What happened to the bullet? Did they have to dig it out?'

He frowned, as though my choice of phrase would not have been his.

'Actually, the bullet went in at the back of your shoulder and came out below your collar-bone, which it missed. You have been very lucky. However, in view of the extent of the wounding it was thought best to keep you from moving about.'

'My left arm feels as though it wouldn't care to try moving itself about. Is that likely to be permanent?'

'I'm told not. The recovery of function should be complete provided there are no arthritic complications.'

I felt it best not to ask about the arthritic complications, though I was sure Mackenzie would have been able to answer any queries on the matter, being fully informed, as part of his duty to a client. While I took a rest he closed the file he had been working on, sliding this back into the suitcase from which he produced a pad he placed on top of his temporary desk. He put spectacles back on his nose and looked at me.

'I haven't yet asked how you are feeling, Miss McLinn?'

'I wouldn't want to scrub the kitchen floor.'

'Ah. Well, fortunately that sort of thing has been taken care of. I have been out to 'Morvern' and I took it upon myself to make certain arrangements, since there was no one else to do this.'

'I hope your arrangements didn't give Aline an active role? She'd be likely to burn the house down.'

'I wouldn't be so foolish as to involve that young lady in anything involving responsibility. A Miss Edna McLeish has volunteered her services. As temporary housekeeper-help.'

A feeling of surprise didn't last long. Edna, established in my house, would be first with the news about any developments in the exciting case of Sophia McLinn, spinster of the parish, and of moderately unsullied reputation, having been shot at with intent to kill up on Ben Tala moor. It was unlikely that Loch Riddoch had been offered a story anything like as enticing since that one about the gamekeeper who had got rid of his wife with an axe, and that must have been about the time of World War One, if not before. I wouldn't just be a nine days' wonder in the village, but a real celebrity certain to be pointed out to visitors for years to come. I considered the prospect for a good minute before I asked:

'Has this got into the papers?'

'It has,' Mackenzie announced. 'And not just the Scottish ones. The London Sundays have been interested, too. I think the use of a helicopter in the matter attracted them.'

'The use of a *what*?'

He might have been watching my face for any revealing changes of expression.

'They brought you down from the mountain in one of those rescue machines that are always kept handy to collect up the English who don't believe that we have serious rock-climbing up here. You were landed right in front of the hospital. It caused quite a sensation. We had seven reporters in the town yesterday wanting the story. The police referred them to me.'

'What did you say?'

'That I had no information to give them beyond the bare facts they already knew. They were difficult to get rid of but I had the advantage in that when I said I knew nothing of what lay behind the shooting incident I was telling the truth.'

Mackenzie was clearly now teetering on the edge of a whole list of questions to me and I held him momentarily by one of my own.

'How did the police know to come after me?'

'As I said just now, Miss McLinn, you have been very

lucky. The man you were supposed to be rescuing up on that moor turned up at your house not much more than half an hour after you had left it. And just at the time the police were returning to 'Morvern' that young American from a questioning in the police station. I understand that your friend had been having some Chinese jar or pot valued for you in Edinburgh. Is that right?'

'Yes.'

'Well, very sensibly he came back to Loch Riddoch via Taybridge and the main road.'

Geoffrey might be living dangerously for him these days but not dangerously enough to risk the high moors when there was a snow warning out. I had been a fool, something that it is particularly depressing to have to accept when you are confined to bed. I lay there, feeling my wound even though I didn't move, wondering if the reason why the bullet had hit my shoulder instead of my head was that just as the killer was about to pull the trigger he had heard a police car coming. That would have been enough to botch even a marksman's shot, suddenly making getting away his top priority. I owed my life to Geoffrey turning up at my house bearing Mother's Chinese bowl, and just when he did. If he had gone up to the hotel for a drink or a cup of tea before bringing me the news about whether the thing was Ching or Tang, I would now be very dead indeed. It was one of those little chances in life which give you furiously to think. It might even be Fate pushing Geoffrey and me together. I closed my eyes on the thought.

'Are you all right, Miss McLinn?'

I didn't open them.

'Just tired.'

It was a moment before he put the question I had been dreading.

'The police asked me to find out if you can give a description of the man who shot you?'

I understood why he had been allowed in alone to see me, a constable or sergeant along with him might be expected to frighten me back into speechless unconsciousness. Friend of the family Mackenzie stood a better chance of getting a statement out of me, or so they thought. Actually my lawyer was showing signs of impatience again.

'Miss McLinn, can you identify the man who tried to kill you?'

'No.'

'You mean you'd never seen him before in your life?'

'I can't be sure of that. In fact I'm pretty sure I have seen him before, and quite often. But not wearing a balaclava to hide his face.'

I had my eyes open again. Mackenzie was making notes.

'And how was he dressed?'

'Ski outfit. Black.'

I told my story, and in some detail, but didn't stress the huntsman theme which certainly diminished its credibility. He stopped writing to tell me this.

'The man could have shot you at any time while all that was going on?'

'Not perhaps at any time, but he had plenty of chances which he didn't take.'

'And you have some idea of why he didn't take them?'

'Yes. He wanted me at a decent range. Otherwise it would have been a dirty kill.'

'Miss McLinn!' That was almost a shout.

'I'm sorry. But that's the way it felt. And I *know* that's the way it was.'

There was silence in the side ward. Mackenzie was now wearing the expression of a man whose legal experience has given him an in-depth training in patience, but which I was none the less once again near to exhausting.

'What happened to the hunter?' I asked.

'The *who*? Oh. He got away.'

'Even with the police up there?'

'Yes. He took your car. Managed to get it a good two miles up the road from the quarry. Almost to the pass. The police say he had to be a rally standard driver. As well as being a keen sportsman, which I take it is what you have been trying to suggest?'

'It's what will be in my official statement when I make it. Don't tell me the police car couldn't go where my Austin had gone?'

'It went up there, but not at once. You had to be looked after. And they had to radio for help. They stayed by you until the American arrived.'

'Dean? You mean he came up after the police?'

Mackenzie nodded.

'And they'd ordered him not to. Paid no attention.'

I lay there feeling absurdly pleased, really only half listening while my lawyer told me how the hunter had got away. Quite easily, it seemed, on skis he must have been carrying in the van and transferred to my car. By the time the police reached my Austin the skier was already a distant figure on a hill to the west. Pursuit was impossible. After it had taken me to hospital the helicopter came back over the moors to have a look, but more snow had fallen and they saw nothing, not even ski tracks. The van had been hired, for a cash payment, by someone called Wilson with an Edinburgh address. The address was all right, but no one called Wilson lived there.

'Miss McLinn, do you think it was the man you called the hunter who phoned you himself?'

'Yes.'

'Couldn't it have been an accomplice?'

I thought about that.

'I doubt it. He knew me, you see. He knew how I would react to being told I wasn't on any account to come up that road myself. I was to leave things to the garage man. He knew I wouldn't.'

Mackenzie was busy writing, but he couldn't resist the comment.

'As you say, he must know you well.'

The way he put that gave me a little jerk of fear. The hunter was still out there, perfectly free, unidentified. The lawyer's pen stopped moving.

'There was nothing about that voice on the phone you recognized? Take time to think about that.'

'I don't need to think about it. The answer is no. The voice was a bit blurred, perhaps, but it could have been a complete stranger. I certainly couldn't identify anyone from what I heard during that call.'

'Had you considered, Miss McLinn, that the call might have been made from that public box not half a mile from your house at the cross-roads? And that the man who had rung you simply got in the van and drove up the Ben Tala road only minutes ahead of you.'

'I hadn't considered it, but it obviously makes sense.'

'You didn't think it curious, in view of those fresh tyre marks in front of you, that anyone would choose to use that road in the conditions prevailing?'

'No, of course I didn't, why should I? It's a public road. There are always idiots about to take risks. And a van driver in a hurry could be one of them. Anyway, I was thinking about my friend, in shock, sitting by the wreck of a car he wouldn't leave. Now will you tell *me* something? If the police think I was led up on to the moors by the killer, did anyone in the Loch Riddoch area see a large blue van hanging about waiting to do the luring away? Or haven't they checked on that?'

'They have and the result is negative.'

'Then that means it must have been hidden someplace which gave it access to the Ben Tala road without having to be driven through Loch Riddoch. Believe me, a large

blue van couldn't have passed through our village in
winter without someone seeing it and wondering what it
was up to. Speculation about anything out of the strict
norm is our cold weather pastime.'

'And if the killer was a local man that is something he
would have had in mind?'

'Certainly.'

'If you're right, that certainly narrows down the search
area. You realize that there will have to be a statement
directly to the police, when you're stronger. Perhaps
tomorrow. I should imagine they will want to know, first,
whether you can offer any possible motive for this crime
and, second, if from that motive you can perhaps guess at
the identity of the man in the ski outfit. No matter that
you have no actual evidence. They'll be very interested in
what you tell them. And so will I. As your solicitor it
would be best if I knew now what your suspicions are. In
total confidence, of course, with nothing said to the
police meantime. You know you can trust me.'

I might know I could trust him, but trust wouldn't
protect me from an explosion when Mackenzie heard the
name that I put forward as prime suspect. My one idea in
those moments was to postpone big trouble until I was in
a better condition to face up to it. Then one of those
things happened which make me wonder whether,
improbable as it might seem, Sophia McLinn could after
all have a guardian angel. If I don't, who else could have
despatched the hospital matron along the corridor at just
that moment?

The lady made an impressive entrance. She was small
of stature but crackled.

'Now then, Mr Mackenzie, I hope you haven't been
tiring out our patient?'

The crackling moved to my bedside. She lifted my wrist
with one hand and a watch suspended from her left
bosom with the other. The message she got from my heart

seemed to surprise her. I could hear the thumping myself.
My arm was laid back on the coverlet.

'Go now, Mr Mackenzie! At *once*!'

CHAPTER 12

I must admit that I felt poorly after my lawyer had left,
with no appetite for the lunch offered. When I suggested
to the house surgeon, on a visit accompanied by Matron,
that I'd have been in better shape if I'd been left to
manufacture my own blood instead of having somebody
else's pumped into me, the two by my bed looked
knowingly at each other as though my case confirmed
once again that mild delirium could be part of the
recovery phase from post-operative shock.

In the afternoon I asked to see back newspapers,
wanting to know just where I stood as a national celebrity,
but the nurse with the strong arms and the kind of
complexion that comes from too much starch in the diet
and no salads, said that I didn't want to read the papers
just now, that I'd find them difficult to hold up. At this,
irritation flicked me out of semi-torpor and I issued what
almost sounded like a firm order. I wanted yesterday's,
and the day before's, and the day before that's papers.
Nurse left me, was only gone for minutes, then came back
to announce that there were no such papers available in
the hospital, or in all Taybridge, since this had been
refuse collection day.

I was really in no condition to carry on a civil rights
struggle against what looked like an attempt to keep me
sealed off from the world. It was certainly a fact that my
private room was very private indeed, and from the way
sounds of other patients didn't reach me, I had been put a
long distance down a corridor from fellow sufferers. Also,

my room must have been declared out of bounds to those hospital tourists, the semi-convalescent in dressing-gowns, who shuffle about on the hunt for someone with whom to exchange medical horror stories. No strange faces appeared around the corner of my door, admission was for staff only, and a very limited staff. If there was a Ward Sister on duty in the area I didn't see her, and though I heard nothing to suggest a policeman stationed on a chair in the corridor I did have a strong feeling of being under some kind of guard.

Instead of the newspapers I was given a highly contemporary women's magazine featuring an article on how to face up to things if your lover packs his suitcase and goes back to his wife, no doubt helpful to many, but rather far from my current problems. Towards evening I was getting a bit peevish, and when Matron, this time on her own, came for a check-up, I could see that she and my nurse were thinking about sedating me again to give themselves a rest. I spent the time until official lights out watching for syringes being smuggled in from outside, or surreptitiously prepared at the washbasin.

But the next morning was a new day, pain under control in that it was perfectly bearable without drugs to soften it down . . . I had even refused a sleeping tablet . . . and I ate a reasonable breakfast to build myself up for what I knew was coming: a visit from the police. I also made a resolution to be a better patient, which was certainly going to be hard to keep. Nurse and I exchanged somewhat uneasy smiles, but there was little small talk between us, though we did both agree that the snow was now probably over for this winter and she congratulated me on getting through all my scrambled egg. The temperature dropped a little when I asked to see today's papers, but she went off and, after half an hour this time, came back with the *Daily Express* and Matron's personal copy of the *Scotsman*.

I searched them both with great diligence, but there wasn't even the hint of a new instalment of the Sophia McLinn story, and I began to wonder if Mackenzie had exaggerated the amount of publicity around my shooting in the hope of bringing me to heel, thinking that someone with my decidedly middle-class background would cringe away from the idea of having my name flashed about in print. Actually, I would have thought so, too, and was somewhat surprised that I wasn't having this reaction. It was as though I had been lying there, with the idea not remote from the edges of my thoughts, that in a depression year, and in an age which dotes on celebrities of any kind, it wouldn't be at all bad for my boarding-house business that I had been shot and come within inches of death from a bullet. There was even the possibility of having a brochure printed which hinted at the personal history of the proprietress, and if I could fill all my rooms from the end of May to the end of September, plus increase my charges by fifteen per cent above the inflation rate, an old dream of a winter holiday in Tenerife might become a reality.

I was in fact thinking about palm trees when the police arrived, two of them, bringing in their own folding chairs from the passage, and Mackenzie as well to look after my interests. If my lawyer charged an hourly rate there was going to be a grim bill to face up to one of these days, and I didn't think I'd get a discount because of my years.

There was considerable shuffling about arranging chairs, during which Nurse escaped to drink Nescafé, leaving me alone to face rather formal enquiries about how I had endured the night that was behind us. The police force consisted of the sergeant who had inter-rogated me in my own kitchen, and the fresh-faced constable who had called me Mother at the station, now along to take notes of my every significant word. Mackenzie sat just slightly apart from the law, rather nearer to me than he had on his first visit, but still with considerable floor space between us. Missing from the party was Detective-Inspector Wilcott of the mysterious special branch who had done so much to brighten up that session at 'Morvern' with his smiles and one laugh, giving me an appreciative audience to play to.

Sergeant Johnson didn't believe in preambles of any kind; he started in on me at once, though not quite as impressively as the last time. It seemed that his hands needed to be doing something, and that he was a lesser man without a pad and pen.

'Mr Mackenzie has let me see the notes he took of his meeting with you yesterday. There wasn't very much that was new to us in what you told him, but then perhaps you weren't up to really thinking things out. Would that be it?'

'I'm not sure what you mean by thinking things out, Sergeant.'

'Well, more detail perhaps. Something that might give us a lead to the identity of the would-be killer.'

'I'd classify him as killer, not would-be.'

The hands with nothing to do settled on the sergeant's knees.

'That's a very definite statement, Miss McLinn, if you don't mind my saying so. I mean, in view of the fact that you claim to have no clue at all as to the identity of the man who tried to shoot you.'

'I never made any such claim, Sergeant.'

'But according to Mr Mackenzie's notes . . .'

'I don't know what he put in his notes, but what I told him was that I couldn't give a positive identification because of the way the killer was covered up. That is very different from saying that I haven't a clue as to who the man was.'

'From which we are to take it that you *do* have a clue?'

'I think so.'

They were all staring at me, even the young constable over at the wall.

'Then perhaps you'll oblige by letting us know what that clue is?'

If that was a bid for sarcasm it didn't attract much attention. I took as deep a breath as my shoulder allowed, then said:

'I think the man with the gun was Colin Gain.'

There was complete silence for a moment, then Mackenzie jumped up, almost tipping back his chair. The look he directed at me in my high hospital bed was now loaded with venom. I didn't think he was over-reacting. His firm, Premble, McFie, McKay and Mackenzie had factored the Gain estates for the better part of a century. My mother had taken our affairs to the partners solely on the recommendation of the late Mrs Gain of Riddoch House. If what I suspected was true, echoes of this scandal would go on for years in the Taybridge area, its reverberations particularly loud in the legal offices where Mackenzie was now the senior partner, Premble, McFie and McKay all having passed on to whatever rewards heaven reserves for successful country lawyers. But even a solicitor whom you have wounded deeply shouldn't shout in a hospital; mine did.

'This is lunacy! Sergeant, I suggest you pay no attention to whatever Miss McLinn may say in her present state. She has obviously been in shock, and lying here her imagination has just run away with her.'

Sergeant Johnson wasn't going to be told what to think. He suggested that Mackenzie sit down again. My solicitor did that, but at once protested that the constable was not to take notes on babblings from a fevered brain, though these weren't quite his words. The sergeant obliged by telling the young policeman to stop scribbling, then he looked at me.

'You must have some grounds for your suspicions, Miss

McLinn. I'd like to hear them.'

My account of a night drive around Loch Riddoch after dinner in the hotel with Geoffrey didn't take more than five minutes, and during it the sergeant's plain, overworked policeman's face settled into an expression of semi-polite scepticism. He then asked pertinent questions about my identification of the driver of a car seen in waiting in the Riddoch House driveway, and was particularly interested in whether the moments during which my full headlights had been on the man could possibly have been long enough for me to be quite certain I had seen Colin Gain.

I said I was *quite* certain, and had at once been curious because our Laird was supposed to be in Rhodes.

'He *is* in Rhodes,' Mackenzie said loudly. 'I had a letter from him two days ago. From his villa there.'

The sergeant was not impressed by a letter from a Greek villa, and went on to ask me about my eyesight. I don't know whether or not I convinced him that my long vision was still perfect even though I needed reading glasses, for by this time his face had stopped registering his reaction to what I told him, which somehow gave me the feeling that scepticism was fading. He asked for my interpretation of Colin Gain's action in chasing me — if it had been Colin Gain — and I said that for some reason it was vitally important to him that no one knew he was back in Loch Riddoch and a local might have identified him even though he had tried to shield his face. He had to find out who I was.

'Surely, Miss McLinn, he would have had no difficulty in doing that once he caught up with your car? As a local man he would probably have recognized your Austin. And you must have been shown up by his headlights. Are you suggesting that he kept on following you because he meant to kill you then?'

'Yes.'

'I've never listened to such nonsense!' Mackenzie shouted.

The protest received no attention. Johnson was now plugging away to trip me up if he could. Did I think the would-be killer's nerve had failed him at the last minute? I said no, it would have been a dirty kill to push me over a hundred-foot drop on to rocks by the loch shore. Also, you can never be sure you have fatality in a road accident, there is always the chance of your victim surviving to talk unless you are prepared to do a messy follow up, and I didn't think Colin Gain would have been prepared to do that. By this time my solicitor was calling on God to help him. The sergeant ignored that too, egging me on, so I told him what Colin was like during the shooting season up on his moors.

'It doesn't matter what those people may be paying for the privilege of killing his grouse, they have to do it according to the Gain rules or else. Last summer he ordered a Zürich banker off the estate for what the man had been doing to the birds. It seems to me quite logical, Sergeant, that a man who is so fussy about the way his rich guests kill grouse would also be fussy about the way *he* killed people. Which is why I think he switched off those headlights before turning his car around and going back to Riddoch House. To take his time to think out a more sporting way to kill me.'

I expected more shouting from Mackenzie at that, but he wasn't even looking at me, the floor seemed to have his interest.

'And while he was laying these careful plans, Miss McLinn, what was to prevent you from going to the police with your account of being chased on a night road?'

I smiled at the sergeant.

'I think you're forgetting just how well our Laird, for all he winters in Rhodes, knows his people in Loch Riddoch. He certainly knows that there is no love lost between me

and the local constable and about the last thing I would
be likely to do is rush down to the village police station
with my story of being chased. It would be the big laugh
in the pub for a week.'

'Very well. So this man knows you wouldn't go to the
police. Why were you a threat to him?'

'Because I was a loose end lying around. And the more
he thought about it, the more dangerous that seemed.
Whatever he is covering up is something very important
to him. It has to be. He's prepared to kill to keep that
cover. As you say, no threat from me going to the police,
at least at first. But supposing my curiosity grew and I
started asking questions in our village, about whether
anyone had seen Colin Gain? Was he back, and so on? As
a matter of fact I did ask just that question. And it's quite
possible he heard that I had.'

'Are you suggesting that he has his own information
service in Loch Riddoch?'

'He could do.'

'Miss McLinn, it really is quite astonishing the way you
have built up a case in your own mind against Mr Gain.
And without being able to offer anything like positive
identification, or even one shred of evidence against him.'

There was a moment's silence. Mackenzie looked up
from the floor. He had already written the letter, on a
clean white sheet in his brain, informing me that his
services were no longer available to me.

'I think I can suggest where you might find just a shred
of evidence,' I said.

'And where would that be, Miss McLinn?'

'Riddoch House. If Colin has been using it quite often
when he was supposed to be in Rhodes, there may be
some traces of that occupation. Perhaps up in an attic
room he could blackout easily. And he'd have to cook.
I've heard that no one ever goes into the house in winter
to clean or anything like that. They have a big blitz just

before the paying guests arrive. I do much the same thing myself.'

'On the evidence you have offered,' the sergeant said. 'Any request I might make for a search warrant would be refused.'

'But you don't need a search warrant,' I told him. 'As factor to the Gain Estates I'm sure that Mr Mackenzie has a key to the place. The visit could be completely unofficial.'

I found the patter of rain against the black square of the window almost sinister. There was wind, too, the modern concrete block of the hospital under a night assault from it. In my too hot, double-glazed cell the spring storm should have been padded away from me, but every now and then someone opened a door, which banged shut again, and after that there was a stirring along corridors, flurries of cooler, moving air which reached my bed as little announcements that even this fortress could be breached.

For most of the day I had been able not to think about Colin Gain, but now I was doing it, and it was almost as though, in allowing him into my mind, I had given him some kind of power which he was exercising. He wanted to be seen in my brain's eye, putting the pictures there, and in a tidily organized sequence.

At twelve he was already the young Laird, his father killed in France, his mother continuing to live in a world that even then had gone, of life subject to the disciplines of the station into which you were born. World War Two may have seemed to put paid to that completely, but there were places in which it continued to survive, particularly in the Scottish Highlands. Mrs Gain had certainly done her best to keep her fragment of the old order alive and flourishing. My mother would never have admitted this, but the *grande dame* of Riddoch House

had condescended to the McLinns, something obvious to
me even when I was quite young, rating us as suitable to
have to afternoon tea from time to time, but certainly
never to dinner.

At those afternoon parties for the socially less fortunate
Colin often made an appearance, though it was no more
than that, almost offering us his considered contempt. I
can remember looking up from easily the world's smallest
tomato sandwich to see him standing in the drawing-
room door wearing a polite smile. That was all he did,
just stood there without a word for perhaps a whole
minute before withdrawing as quietly as he had arrived.
Once when I was there his mother had called out to him
to come and join us, her voice sharpish, but all he did was
finish off his smile, then turn, the door clicking shut. Mrs
Gain had said something about the dear boy with so
much on his mind at the moment.

I can remember the youth's face as well as the man's. It
didn't seem to change all that much, as though aging had
been a matter of becoming sterner with himself. He
might even have had a clear picture of the role he wanted
to play, the military man back from the wars spending
some time in the family home among his faithful
peasants. Not quite that, perhaps, but not so far off it; to
me everything he did was a pose, his gracious affability to
'his people' in the village, the military bearing which had
no more to do with soldiering than his short back and
sides haircut, Colin somehow avoiding all the minor wars
that would certainly have been available had he wanted
to see action. He drove fast cars well and had done some
rallying and was certainly a first-class shot. Just where
lotus-eating on Rhodes fitted into all this I couldn't quite
see, but then strong sun does change people almost the
moment they move under it, as I knew myself from my
time in Italy.

Lying in that hospital bed, and feeling pretty helpless

still, the last thing I wanted to do was think about unfinished business between Colin and me, but my brain refused to accept a switch-off on the theme. Whatever Sergeant Johnson might have found in Riddoch House after Mackenzie had opened up for him, I didn't think it would be the Laird camping out in one of his own attic bedrooms. After what had happened up on the Ben Tala moor he wouldn't return to an old hide, but I didn't think that would leave him with no place to go. No one knew those hills better than he did, he owned huge stretches of them, and it didn't seem to me at all improbable that he had considered the possibility of an emergency and made plans to meet it. A reserve hide would be easy enough for him to fix up, it could be a disused shepherd's cottage up a remote glen or a caravan on an isolated site ostensibly belonging to townees who rarely visited it.

It must have been that first bullet fired in my direction from a 303 which had convinced me that Colin Gain wanted me dead because I was a threat to the careful cover he had built up for some criminal activity. The idea that Loch Riddoch's top man was operating outside the law certainly hadn't come as the kind of shock likely to keep me from sleeping. What wasn't so easy to push from a mind perhaps made a bit feverish by a post-operative temperature was the thought that he had twice come near to getting rid of me and that third time tended to be lucky.

Loch Riddoch House might offer the police evidence that Colin had been living there in recent days, but it seemed unlikely that they would come on pointers to anything more than that, and if I wasn't around to testify in court there would just be no way in which they could make stick a charge of attempted murder. If he was able to silence me, then get out of the country, it wouldn't be easy to challenge his alibi that he had been living happily on Rhodes since the end of the last Scottish grouse-shooting season. Probably no one would try to, but even if they did, and from what I'd heard about his lifestyle out on the Greek island, there would be a whole posse of well paid serfs to support his claim.

All this must have occurred to Colin while I was still on the operating table, and I didn't care for the idea of him in a reserve hide somewhere keeping tabs on how I was doing. He mightn't have had access to press accounts of the moor shooting, but he would certainly have a radio, and the Scottish news on it must have given him at least the information that I wasn't dead and possibly that I was off the danger list and doing nicely.

In spite of all this I did sleep, or at least doze, waking from a spell of doing that to a dim light by my bed and a bluish glow from the corridor. Somewhere at a good distance there was a coughing, probably from a patient in the main ward, but otherwise, except for gusts of wind against the window, it was still and very hot. I was using my good hand to pull down the coverlet when cool air reached me. This was much stronger than those daytime flurries I had felt when someone had opened a door to the outside; this time it was a real blast of cold air which made me decide to leave the coverlet where it was. It could be one of the walking wounded seeking an escape from the torrid hospital heat and certainly whoever it might be stood in the opening for a good five minutes. I didn't hear a door or window being shut, but slightly hissing radiators fought the invasion and defeated it. I was half expecting to hear the sound of slippered feet coming along the corridor past my open door, but this didn't happen.

It must have been all of ten minutes later when I knew there was someone in my room. I had been lying with my eyes shut and hadn't consciously heard anything, but was still certain I was being watched from just inside the door. I remembered a pushbell on the wall near the bed. I had never used it and wasn't sure I could reach it quickly with my good arm.

I tried to tell myself it was the night nurse come to check up on me, but couldn't believe she would have moved so silently. If I opened my eyes whoever was there would see that. If I reached for the bell there would be a quick crossing of the little room to the bed.

I had to look. There was a shape by the door, almost like a flat shadow pinned back against the wall. It didn't move. I had the feeling that I wouldn't be able to scream, that the sound would be choked inside my own body. I had never known such helplessness, the victim who could do nothing.

'Miss McLinn . . . ?'

The whisper was so low I almost thought I'd imagined it. Then it was repeated, my name a little louder, as though whoever was there had to have some sign from me. I didn't move.

The shadow did, just a step forward to where the blue light from the hall gave it shape, lengthening it into a man, too tall for a woman. It was too tall to be Colin Gain. I knew who he was.

'Dean!'

He might have been afraid of a body on the bed, of having to look at it, from the way he stopped half way to me in a zone of near-darkness between the blue glow from the corridor and the dim night light above my pillows.

'I had to come,' he said. 'They wouldn't let me in.'

I whispered that he was to come round to the other side of me where there was a chair. If the night nurse came he could hide under the high bed. She wouldn't put on a bright light. I asked what their excuse had been at hospital reception not to let him see me.

'You couldn't see people, that's all. No reason. I couldn't find out a damn thing!'

'Keep whispering, Dean.'

'Sure. You okay? Really?'

'Except for a hole in my shoulder.'

'Oh God, I know! I was there. You were bleeding on the snow. I couldn't do anything. The police couldn't either. You never made a sound, even when the 'copter came in. It couldn't land because of the slope, so you had to be winched up on a stretcher. It felt like it took about a week. I thought you'd had it, sure. Can I get a drink of water?'

He was careful to make no noise with the tap. He drank at the basin, then crossed to the door to look down the corridor before coming back to the seat.

'I phoned your lawyer yesterday. He admitted he'd been in to see you, but that was all. He wouldn't tell me one damn thing about you. I got the picture that you were alive, that's all. How alive I didn't know. That guy thinks I could be the killer of Murdo, doesn't he?'

'I don't know, Dean.'

'Am I tiring you? Just tell me and I'll go.'

'How did you get in here?'

'Fire escape. Not easy. You got to jump and do a trapeze act at the start. I had to jump twice, the first one wasn't good enough. Can you move this hand at all?'

'Yes. But it doesn't like it.'

'You know who that bastard who shot you was, don't you?'

'I think so.'

'Tell me and I'll go after him.'

'I'm not telling you.'

'That's a relief,' I could just see him grinning at me. 'Are the police on to anything?'

'I don't know. Are they leaving you alone?'

'Sure. As long as I stay quiet in the village. They wouldn't be too happy to know I'd got as far as this with no bleep on their radar screens. I wouldn't have done in my car, I can tell you that. So it's still parked in front of your house. I pushed your bike across fields to get clear of the village, then rode on in here. Never stopped. These days, if you're on a bike you got to be an innocent.'

'Won't they know in "Morvern" you're away?'

'How? Aline and me don't talk. That Edna goes home at night after cooking horrible meals. To paste up her scrapbook.'

'What?'

'She's keeping it on you. One of the tabloids called you "victim of the snow killer". How about that? But the story's dead now. I told Edna it wouldn't hold for more than a couple of days. Not unless the killer strikes again. God, I feel a lot better. Even after playing ape on that fire escape.'

'And all those miles on a bicycle.'

'Yup. I couldn't bring you flowers.'

There were footsteps in the corridor. Dean remembered his emergency drill.

By my assessment the night duty nurse was well past retiring age, back doing shift work to pay for running her car. She had trained in the days when nursing was a vocation, taught that patients were there to be disciplined, not coddled. Whatever she might have been told about me she wasn't prepared to stand any nonsense. The approach to my bed was made with hands on her hips.

'I thought I heard voices in here?'

'You probably did,' I told her. 'Since the police aren't allowing me any friendly visitors I've taken to talking to myself.'

CHAPTER 13

Mackenzie brought me my first flowers, six daffodils and three red tulips, indicators that spring was about to hit us and also that, in spite of harsh words flying about recently, I was still his client. This could only mean that the sergeant and he had found something interesting at Riddoch House. I was itching to hear about it, but contrived to show patience.

My lawyer pulled his chair half way across towards my bed, something almost symbolic in this. He had come without that huge attaché case from which he could produce an assortment of the paraphernalia of his trade, notebooks, files and probably, if needed, a sizeable tome on Scottish law. Without the backing of his portable office he somehow looked vulnerable.

'Miss McLinn, I want to apologize for anything said in haste yesterday. I certainly should not have spoken as I did. But I'm sure you'll appreciate that what you suggested came to me like a bolt from the blue.'

A slight warming towards the man meant I could forgive him the cliché. And in his case it was probably appropriate. If they had found any pointers towards Colin as the gunman it would certainly be stunning to the Gain estate's factor. No doubt a considerable portion of the firm's income, which meant Mackenzie's income, had come from this source. I could see that he'd had an even more disturbed night than mine.

'There was no way I could put things gently,' I said.

He nodded. I decided to plunge right in.

'Have they caught Colin?'

He shook his head.

'But they believe now he shot me?'

This time he nodded.

'Why?' I asked.

'The police have arrested a man who was one of Gain's assistants. He's confessed.'

'What man? And what's he confessed to?'

'Heroin smuggling,' Mackenzie said. 'He's your local garage man at Loch Riddoch.'

Jock! And as sure as anything that meant Murdo, too. It wasn't exactly news to me. I remembered Aline coming back from a meeting that had almost certainly been with Jock to get more of the drug. I should have done something about that then, reported it probably. But there would have been no proof, just suspicion, and you can't sell suspicion to the police in the country, they're surrounded by it all the time.

'It's all pretty horrible,' Mackenzie said, in a non-professional voice. 'And going on for years. Seven years!'

He didn't elaborate on that with any bid then for sympathy on what this was going to mean to him personally. It couldn't but mean a lot. When the news got out in the Taybridge district even the generous-hearted would be saying it was curious that the factor of the Gain estate had never had the slightest inkling of what the proprietor had been up to by way of criminal activities. And what the non-generous would be saying didn't bear thinking about. Country lawyers really can't afford to have crooked clients, especially when these clients represent a fair portion of their business. As a semi-impoverished boarding-house-keeper who would now stick with Mackenzie through the dark days ahead I deserved my daffodils and three tulips.

I asked a question which had certainly been on my mind. 'Are the police still looking for Colin in this area?'

'Yes. But he seems to have vanished.'

'Can't our garage man give them a lead?'

'I just don't know what may have come out of that

questioning, Miss McLinn. I rang Sergeant Johnson this morning, but he wasn't very forthcoming.'

Which could be the first sign of barriers about to go up against Mackenzie. I must not allow myself to begin to feel sorry for a member of the legal profession; they all look after each other well enough. I asked what had happened when he went to Riddoch House with the sergeant and his account was economical but quite clear.

They hadn't gone to the Gain estate after the session with me; Mackenzie had to be in Perth for the rest of the day and didn't get back until late evening, when he found Johnson had gone out to a serious road accident. I rather gathered that Mackenzie had been quite happy to go to the house in the dark, the later the better. He didn't care for the idea of being seen escorting the police over a client's home. It was nearly eleven when they got out there and someone else had also decided to take advantage of a dark night; a torch flashed in an attic bedroom just as the police car came up the drive. They caught Jock lying sprawled at the foot of the grand staircase with a badly twisted ankle. He had missed his step while on the way at speed towards a motor-bike parked under a window that had been forced. In the inner pockets of his poacher's jacket were four bags of what he claimed to be sugar, one of them burst open. The sergeant sniffed and tasted the stuff and pronounced it heroin.

'To say that the garage man squealed then would be to use the right word,' Mackenzie announced. 'His voice went almost falsetto. I have never run into anyone prepared to turn Queen's evidence so fast. In a couple of minutes he had incriminated Gain as the head of the operation, with the dead Menzies as his local second-in-command, plus two distributors in Taybridge and three suspects in Perth.'

Mackenzie paused, and for a moment I thought it was

going to be to let me know that the Taybridge police would be forever in my debt for the lead I had given them, but my part in all this had apparently been completely forgotten, the swoop on Riddoch House now being attributed to male investigative intuition. Life is not just unfair, you have to get out and kick it to make it take any notice of you, and just then I still wasn't up to kicking anything. I just lay and listened.

Jock had talked all the way in the car bringing them back to town, but from what Mackenzie had heard it didn't look as though he was going to be much help in the hunt for Colin Gain. Though the garage man had serviced most of the estate vehicles, and Colin would stop sometimes to fill the tank of his BMW, there was never a hint of heroin smuggling in these contacts, Jock got his orders from Murdo Menzies, never direct. That is, until Murdo's body was washed up, when there was contact, a phone call from Colin to arrange a rendezvous. Jock didn't know whether this was to discuss his promotion into Murdo's job, or merely for a handout of the supplies he used to get through Murdo. He needed those supplies badly and had come to Loch Riddoch House because Colin never kept his appointment.

Or that was his story. I didn't think, for all Jock's squealing to the police, that it was the whole story, and said so to the lawyer.

'What do you mean?'

'There was another phone call from Colin to Jock,' I said. 'At least, I'm pretty sure there must have been. And not about a meeting between them. Part of the arrangements to get rid of me.'

'What? Are you suggesting the garage man was an accessory?'

'Yes. Hard to prove, but it might provoke Jock to even more useful squealing if the police sprang it on him suddenly. You see, I'm certain that Colin must have rung

Jock's garage just before the call to me that got me up on to Ben Tala. Colin insisted then, playing the commercial traveller, that my stranded friend didn't want me to come up there myself, just to get in touch with the garage to have Jock come up in the breakdown. Colin would never have told me that if he hadn't been dead sure I would get no answer when I rang the garage. And been equally sure that I'd come myself. Also, I can't believe that Jock and Colin never met. They must have. Wouldn't it have been Jock who brought back his boss from Rhodes after Murdo had been missing for three weeks? Mightn't it be that he's trying to distance himself from Colin this way now because he's even more frightened of him than he is of the police?'

Mackenzie considered my suggestions, then came to a cautious reaction to them.

'Interesting,' he said.

'You could try feeding it to the police.'

He nodded.

'I might just do that, Miss McLinn. And thank you.'

So I got my thanks, though they never became official. My lawyer stood.

'Now I must away, or I'll be tiring you. You haven't any ideas as to where Gain might be hiding?'

'I think he's gone,' I said. 'Long ago he must have had a hide prepared against the day when things started to go wrong. Somewhere no one would think of looking for him. Another country, but not one of the playgrounds. The States, perhaps? Say Philadelphia?'

'Why Philadelphia?'

'It's a city. Only a fool tries to hide in the country. Colin would know it can't be done. How long has he been working the heroin trade?'

'About seven years.'

'So he'll be rich?'

Mackenzie surprised me then.

'Very,' he said. 'The bastard!'

I had an afternoon visit from Dean. He was wearing jeans, a tartan wool shirt open at the neck and something of the look of a man who is just waiting to be redeemed by the love of a good woman. A bandage around the palm of one hand, covering a gash received during his descent of the hospital fire-escape, only made him look more interesting. My slightly spotty nurse clearly thought him the most beautiful thing she had seen in years, but if Dean noticed her at all he gave no sign of this. Texan generosity had made his flowers a dozen and a half daffodils and nine red tulips.

A second visit so soon after the first could only mean that he had things to talk over. He gave me the good news first.

'I had a phone call from your police.'

From the way he said that I could have been District Commissioner of the Force.

'What about?'

'I guess the heat's off. On account of their finding that bike this morning.'

'What bike?'

'That shit Murdo's. Sorry.'

'A motor-bike, was it?'

'That's right. Twenty-five feet down under water. But still carrying its payload.'

'Which was heroin?' I suggested.

'Sure. Saddlebags full of the stuff. Under fishing gear. That's what he used to do, I guess. Pretend he was going fishing. Rod and all the stuff tied on the bike. Meant he could be away for days and it was just Murdo gone fishing again. Neat. The stuff was in sugar sacks. Most of them got bust and the heroin washed out, but enough for the tests. Half the village was down there watching when they heard the bike was about to come up. Big thrill. Been better, though, if Murdo'd still been in the saddle. Edna was there. Came back red-eyed from crying. Had a wonderful time.'

Somehow Dean's late-afternoon cynicism didn't sit on him too well.

'You heard about the garage guy?' he asked.

'Yes.'

'That's where Aline was getting the speed. That is, when Murdo wasn't around to hand it to her.'

'How is she?'

'Strung out. Withdrawal from the joy juice. I've seen it before. She's quit the stuff about eighteen times in the last year. Edna and I try to keep the kid from her. Though she wants to go on feeding him. It's weird. But Edna's got Pete on some stuff she says made her what she is. They ought to put her on television. I can't understand half of what she says, but we get on all right. But what a cook, everything burnt. It's like being back at summer camp. She goes home at night, to look after what she calls her old Mum. I got a feeling she wouldn't mind staying to look after me. She really hates Aline.'

It certainly sounded remote from the usual winter peace and quiet at 'Morvern'.

'When did you hear from the police?' I asked.

'Just after what Edna calls dinner. When she makes her big effort. It was your local cop who came. With instructions from the ones who matter in Taybridge. You could see he'd been told to handle me real gentle. I wasn't to get the idea they'd ever thought I shot Murdo. Nothing like that. All I'd had served me was the questions everyone else was getting. Like hell! Maybe they're scared at the idea of an American suing the Scotch police for damages. That would really get in the papers. Anyway, they're sorry if I was sort of upset at the idea of being watched. I was to understand that following me from Aberdeen that day was just routine police tailing practice. Or something. It looked like I really had that little guy on the run, so I asked a few questions. Like who they *now* thought had killed Murdo. You know the answer to that? Same guy that shot you. The local Mr Big. Shocking thing when you can't count on your aristocrats even staying pure.'

'Colin Gain was no aristocrat. Just third generation money.'

'Oh. Is that all? Back home third generation money is practically God.'

'Why do the police think Colin would want to kill his own number two?'

'Maybe number two starts pushing towards being number one. It happens all the time. Or Murdo could have been threatening a strike to get his heroin pay-off inflation proofed. Anyway, I don't give a damn about police theories, just so long as they let me right out.'

'Are you going to try to get your job on the rig back?'

'I have. After the village cop left I rang Aberdeen. They weren't listening. Place filled already. So then I rang Dallas.'

There was a shudder through my brain at the thought of the phone bill.

'Better luck in America?'

'It's in Mexico. A drilling rig. One of these self-powered jobs on an oil hunt. They can get me on it if I can get over there fast enough.'

The reason for a second visit so soon after the first was now perfectly plain. He didn't have to ask the question, it had reached me by telepathy and my answer was 'no' punctuated by two exclamation marks. Dean left his chair and went over to the window to stand looking out at a Scotland moving into a spring that could still feel very like winter.

'I got no right to ask this, Miss McLinn.'

'Agreed,' I said.

That made him turn.

'Look, I know what you're thinking. But it isn't so bad as that.'

'Probably worse,' I told him.

'Now listen to me, please, just one minute. Aline's strung out right now, see? Before you're out of hospital that'll be over. I'm getting her registered with a doctor as an addict.'

'So she gets the drug legally?'

'Only a controlled amount, Miss McLinn. As part of a cure. It's what she's always needed. I mean the discipline of a doctor saying how much she can have. And taking her off it slow. There's no way after what's happened that she's going to get any extra stuff in these parts. Which is why I want her to stay. Go to a city and she's had it.'

'Dean, are you still in love with her?'

'Oh God, I dunno.'

He did know. He just wasn't letting himself see it.

'How much time did Dallas give you before you have to leave for this job?'

He turned to look out of the window again.

'They said get your ass over here this week if you want it.'

Nurse came in with the daffodils and the tulips. She was uncertain about where the vase should go. Wherever she put it the Dean collection contrived to sneer at the Mackenzie's. Nurse and I had a little chat about how beautiful the flowers were while all the time she kept throwing glances towards a beautiful back at the window. For a moment I thought she was going to clean the washbasin again as an excuse to be near him. As her footsteps faded down the corridor Dean continued to stare at the view as though he was trying to implant a negative of this vista in his brain for total recall when an old man.

'Edna says you have a hired girl in the summer,' he

announced suddenly.

'That's right. For general housework and some scrubbing. These days you have to go easy on the scrubbing or they won't come. So I do most of that myself.'

'What about the cooking?'

He still wasn't turning from the view.

'I do that myself, too, such as it is. And if you are going to suggest Aline for the housework and the scrubbing, that's out. From what I've seen of her she wouldn't take to either.'

Dean swung round.

'You could *make* her.'

I stared at him.

'Even if I could, why should I? I'm not running some kind of rehabilitation clinic. Just a boarding-house offering cold meat and salad high teas and the big excitement of going to bed with a porcelain hot-water bottle. Also, there is the fact that Aline doesn't like me, and I respond to that. Not seeing her is one of the few things I really enjoy about being in hospital.'

'Then I guess it'll have to be Tania,' Dean said.

'Who?'

'The girl Aline was living with in London. They had an apartment. Tania didn't want Aline to come away with me. She said we'd be cat and dog in a month.'

I couldn't risk relaxing my defences with this boy.

'How long before that actually happened?' I asked.

'I guess you could say three months.'

'And you've been dragging things out ever since?'

'Well, it wasn't always like that. Not when I'd get back from the rig at first. It was good for a couple of days, maybe. Then she'd be on speed again. Not just boosters, either. So you'd really notice. I'd have to take over looking after the kid. Though she'd always feed him.'

I didn't want to let my mind play with pictures of

Dean's life with Aline. The miracle, if you could call it that, was that he still felt under any obligation to the girl. From what I could see, all he had got out of their relationship had been three relatively good months followed by semi-hell. Pete was in no way his responsibility, and I couldn't feel that there had been any growth of affection between them. He certainly didn't behave like an adoptive father, just did the duty there that had been shoved at him, as he did the other duties shoved at him. It wasn't cynical to believe that nine hundred and ninety-nine men in a thousand, caught in Dean's circumstances, would simply have packed suitcases and left, leaving no forwarding address. Yet he had seriously considered going to the awful lengths of marrying her, though that idea was fading, if it hadn't gone altogether.

He gave up the view, but from his expression as he came back to the chair, still wasn't satisfied that he had managed to stamp every detail of it indelibly on his retinas.

'What was Tania like?' I asked.

He sat down to consider this.

'Sort of potent, I guess.'

'What does that mean?'

'A kind of earth mother.'

Perhaps I looked puzzled.

'You know, all sorts of beads and long skirts,' he explained. 'She wasn't skinny. She had a kid, too.'

'How about men?'

'Except at parties it was all girls together. I see that now.'

He pushed back his chair while still sitting on it.

'Look, Miss McLinn, forget everything I said. I got no right to come here asking can I dump things on you. I got to say this, though. It wasn't going to be just that. I mean, I was going to pay. And as soon as I got time off from the

Mexico job I'd have been coming back over here. Probably in the fall.'

He stood.

'All you got to do is get better,' he told me.

He had dismissed a wild hope. I didn't want to meet his eyes.

'What are you going to do now, Dean?'

'Go on back to your house and pack up. Get all our stuff in the Fiat and go to London. Tania'll take her in. If there's money coming with her.'

I could see that emigration from Loch Riddoch, the laden small car on the motorway, the family unit minus everything that makes a family unit, silence between the two in front and probably silence, too, from Pete nested and solitary among the luggage, en route to the earth mother.

'Thanks for everything,' Dean said. 'I guess I'm owing you a lot more money. I'll be writing about that. Just now I got to sort things out. And from here on keep out of the way of guys with guns.' He walked towards the door and there raised a hand. 'See you.'

'Dean! Come back!'

'What?'

'I said come back in here!'

'Sure.'

He came to the other side of the bed and stood there. 'So?'

'We have a travel agency in Taybridge. It'll still be open. Go in there and book yourself a seat back to the States from Prestwick. Fly tomorrow if you can. Aline and Edna can fight it out until I get home. After that I'll keep Aline for the summer. And, dammit, she'll learn to scrub!'

He stared down.

'You don't mean this! Anyway, I'm not going to let you do it!'

But he would. He knew it, and so did I.

CHAPTER 14

It wasn't the police who found Colin Gain, it was Geordie McFie and his dog Nell. The shepherd had gone up on to high ground to look for one of his sheep which had always preferred the grass at altitudes above two thousand feet. The beast did solo climbs to reach this, foolhardy and a loner, for whose survival this time there was really no hope after that late blizzard and the hard frost following. The sheep was dead and so was Colin.

Loch Riddoch's laird had died fighting. The light must have been fading when he came down a steep gradient and failed to identify a long ridge in the snow as a stone wall. That he had hit this at speed was obvious, he had broken a ski as well as his right leg in two places. He must have been in agony as he set about his survival project, building himself a shelter in the lee of the stone dyke, using the skis as supports for the wall of rounded bricks made from snow that would have frozen almost as he shaped them. There was no way of knowing how long he had lived inside that lair; he certainly hadn't attempted to break out of it, and further snowfalls finished off the roof over him, making a white hump which survived the thaw that brought Geordie up the mountainside.

It was a slow way to die. From the position of the body it almost looked as though he had arranged himself neatly in that temporary tomb, the shattered leg stretched out as straight as it could be, arms at his sides. There would have been periods of total consciousness towards the end and he must have lain there knowing finally that no escape was possible, feeling death creep up on him, the numbing cold an anæsthetic against pain but also its signature. I found myself almost wishing him a kind of peace at the end, but Sergeant Johnson was pitiless.

'They should be stamped on, all that lot! There's some that think they've a right to money. Like God meant them to have it. And when it isn't coming in to their families like it used to, from sweating the workers, they go all out to get it any way they can. And to hell with the rest of us.'

The sergeant had to be an incomer from industrial Scotland, over the years successfully resisting becoming infected by the natural conservatism of the Highlands. It was pretty obvious the way he would vote at the next election. But perhaps a boarding-house-keeper automatically qualified as a worker of the world; he was certainly being remarkably gracious, the visit almost social, as though he felt he had to make amends for the tone of our previous contacts.

'You'll have wondered, Miss McLinn, why Gain needed to hire that van in Perth?'

'A hearse for me, wasn't it?'

'Aye, you're right. And to carry his skis. He hired them in Perth as well. That man thought of everything. When you think what he'd been getting away with for years. The local laird! About the best cover you could get.'

'Sergeant, have you any idea how he brought the heroin into the country?'

'We do not. And if you ask me we never will. In spite of that inspector up from England. Remember, he was in your kitchen that day?'

'I remember.'

'Aye, well he'd been on the job up here for a couple of months at least.'

'Getting near to Colin Gain?'

'I wouldn't say that. He might, but *I* wouldn't. Though, mind you, it's been interesting. What he found out. Interesting for them down in England, that is. We already knew. At least we'd a good idea.'

'Of what?'

'How the heroin was getting here. Not up from the south at all. It was exported south from us. We're wide open for the trade, and I mean wide open. The inspector was in Dundee first, sniffing about the jute boats from Pakistan. Then he moves up the coast from there. What's he find? Surprise, surprise, what we could have told him easy enough if he'd asked us. That there's at least twenty-five wee harbours on the east coast of Scotland where boats from the Continent can come in with nobody asking them their business. And no coastguard or Customs' man ever comes near them to find out what they're up to. You ask why? I'll tell you. It's this government's damned economies. There just aren't enough men to cover the wee places. Take Customs. You'll find one man has three-four harbours to look after. And maybe a pushbike to get between them. As for out west, it's wide open. There's hundreds of offshore islands without a living soul on them. Not even sheep. You could land a regiment of Russians and who the hell would know? As for the heroin, it could come ashore in bales. I'll tell you one thing we found out about Gain. It's only three years since your laird sold the thirty-five-footer he used to sail out of Oban. Maybe he decided it was too risky using his own boat. The thing is, he knew both coasts damn well. We found charts in the library at Riddoch House. I tell you, Miss McLinn, the heroin kings are just laughing. And don't tell me he was the only one of his kind up here, because I won't believe it.'

I didn't try to tell the sergeant anything. What he said was probably near enough to the truth. Strange stories float about among us which never reach the national press, probably because they seem too fantastic. I asked a question to which I didn't really expect a straight answer.

'Do the police now think that Colin shot Murdo Menzies?'

The sergeant was in a giving mood.

'Aye, you could say we do. The heroin business is tricky. Big profits, big risks. Especially on the retail side for the risks. And Gain was in both. Supplying and marketing. That is, the marketing through Menzies, which put the number two man right out in front with the risks. And he had to know that his boss was a smooth worker, who would get out from under fast if things looked bad. There's a hundred ways those two could have fallen out. Menzies was a tough character. No need to tell you. You didn't like him all that much, Miss McLinn, did you?'

'No. And I suppose that will be on your files forever.'

He smiled. It was the first time I'd seen him do it.

'Well, maybe. I wouldn't worry about it. But you see what I'm getting at? Menzies wouldn't stand anything he didn't like from the big boss. We'll probably never know what it was, but something happened between those two which made Gain think that Menzies was best dead. Even though he was a key on the distribution side.'

'Does Jock back up that theory?'

'We don't give a damn whether he does or not. I wouldn't say in front of a lady what I think of that one. Dishing it out in Taybridge. You know we've now got thirteen registered addicts? But the big trade was from the visitors. They came because they knew they could get it. It makes you sick. Something you might expect in a place like Glasgow. Or Edinburgh. But not in Taybridge, for God's sake. And the kids coming up. And what can we do with them, eh? Once you could give them a skelp round the earhole when you caught them at the beginning of something. Now you put a hand on them and you're taken to the United Nations in New York. Or maybe it's Luxembourg. I'm not up on these things, and don't want to be. I can tell you this right now: if my force in Taybridge was let to do things in their own way we could stop vandalism in a couple of months. We'd be so pure they'd come to look at us from the south of England as a bloody miracle, if you'll excuse my language.'

'I was in the Women's Army, Sergeant.'

'Oh, I'd forgotten that. Well, we won't get things our own way. And neither did Mr Gain in the end. You know, I wish I'd met him. I never even saw him. He must have come into Taybridge often enough during the summer when he was there, and someone could have pointed him out. But they never did. All I saw was his corpse. He wasn't such a big man, was he? Physically, I mean?'

'No, he wasn't.'

'You knew him quite well, didn't you?'

'Only up to a point.'

'Would you say he was a man for the ladies? There's all kinds of stories about him. Women on that island and whatnot. But it could be just talk, you know. I'd say a man like that was a loner. Has to be if he's keeping things tight. And that's what he did, fooling us all. Kept them tight for years. Well, I must be going. I haven't really asked how you're doing?'

'Well enough. I'll be home soon.'

'Quite a show we put on for you, you'll admit that. I mean, calling in the helicopter. We could never have taken you down in the police car. You'd have been dead. You were bleeding something awful. You're a strong woman.'

'That's what they think in here.'

'I think it, too. Pity you couldn't see all that was happening, though. Up there on the snow.'

'I'm quite pleased I didn't. Tell me something before you go, Sergeant. Did you at any time think I was directly involved in all this? Perhaps with Colin Gain?'

He stood. Again he smiled.

'Well, now, put it like this. I usually start out suspecting everyone within range. You don't often go wrong doing that.'

*

Before the hospital got rid of me there was some talk of a convalescent home for another fortnight, but it wouldn't have been fair on Edna to deny her the chance of looking after me while I was still feeble enough to be liable to make her my confidant. I declined the Health Board invitation and was sent home in an ambulance.

Edna had taken over 'Morvern' with an efficiency I wouldn't have believed possible. I lay in my own bed thinking that I really ought to offer her a partnership in the guest-house business, and that, if I did, I might well end up being able to spend a month each winter at Reid's Hotel in Madeira. Before this happy development, however, I'd have to sink all my capital in refurbishing the old homestead, new bathrooms, central heating, a dimly lit cocktail bar sited in what was now my back sitting-room, and probably chalets on the lawn equipped with plastic-roofed car ports. To the brave come the rewards, but I wasn't sure I had the strength any more to be brave.

In among the mail waiting for me at home, which was mostly gas and electricity bills, was a letter from the managing editor of the *Perthshire Informer* stating with less politeness than I thought I had a right to expect that due to changes in policy they were eliminating 'A Countrywoman's Notes' from their pages. Enclosed was a cheque for twenty pounds offered as insurance against any threat that I might take my case to an industrial tribunal, charging them with unfair dismissal.

In view of my history of all those rejections from other editors it looked as though I must now face the fact that my career in marketable creative writing was at an end. I was doing that, looking up at a ceiling on which the cracks in the plaster seemed to have doubled since last I noticed them, when Edna brought in Peter.

'Here's the boy then,' she said. 'Isn't he getting fat?'

He was, on Bayola. I asked about this and had it confirmed, which for some reason made me a little uneasy, but it shouldn't have done, not with the evidence of the energy that Edna had shown she could switch on when she really had an incentive, which in this case was to show Aline up good and proper once and for all.

I had seen Aline once since my return, ten minutes during which we had, remarkably, even less to say to each other than before I was shot. Pete I had met twice, but this was to be our first *tête-à-tête*. Edna settled the baby on my quilt for the occasion and then left. Pete turned his head to watch her go and I thought he was going to howl. It was perfectly plain whose company he preferred. The speed with which a small child who has seemed to need you can switch to someone else for the satisfaction of those needs is probably the real reason why they survive to become adults. I doubt if the young of any other species have quite the same gift.

It is always salutary, of course, to appreciate the facts but I won't deny that I felt slightly bruised by Pete's obvious indifference to me in view of our past relationship, which had had its moments of considerable intimacy. Perhaps because of this I didn't try to do anything to entertain him, we just sat and looked at each other. His startling violet-coloured eyes weren't any less startling than they had been, but now I couldn't really see them as the visible extensions of what was likely to be a brilliant brain. It just could be that he would evolve into a far from clever child, and from that to an extremely tiresome adolescent. Also, Aline was his mother.

My thoughts had come very close to putting me in a state of unease when there was a sudden change in Pete's expression, the indifference, plus boredom, sliding away, replaced by attention to me, as though my face had just reminded him of something highly entertaining from our mutual past. He showed his gums and made the noise of early laughter.

I reached down. He was quite willing to come. Edna hadn't found time to change him and he was very wet. I got out of bed, put on a dressing-gown, and went across to the bathroom where a row of clean nappies hung on a line over the tub. I was busy with safety-pins above a Pete who seemed relaxed about being serviced by me when the front doorbell rang. The voices I heard through an open door belonged to Edna and Geoffrey, these fading as she showed him into the chilly drawing-room. A minute and a half later she said from my threshold:

'You shouldn't be doing that!'

'Pete thought somebody should. Fast.'

She laughed. 'You know this, I've never liked kids. But I quite like that one. You feel he notices what you does for him. Well, that's something isn't it? You know who it is downstairs?'

'Yes.'

'He's come to see you. I'll give this place a bit of a tidy, then he can come up. Okay?'

'No. I'll go down.'

'What? In that dressing-gown?'

'It doesn't have egg stains.'

'Well, for Gawd's sake, at least comb your hair.'

I went to the dressing-table where the mirror deceived, though it wasn't doing that this afternoon, perhaps due to a setting westerly sun beaming in hard light. Edna was right about my hair and was probably right about the dressing-gown, too, but Geoffrey was still going to see me in it. I used some powder, observed from the area of the bed by two sets of eyes, then got up and left the bedroom. On the stairs I felt just slightly shaky and had to slow down, but revived as I was passing the cigar store Indian to enter the drawing-room as something like three-quarters of my normal self.

Geoffrey had not been to see me in hospital, sending daffodils and a note explaining that the sale of his town house had forced him to be in Edinburgh much of the time even though he had rented a Loch Riddoch Hotel chalet for a month. He was standing now near the windows with his hands out almost touching the Chinese bowl he hadn't been able to turn into a small fortune to comfort my old age. From the way his head was bent he was obviously staring down at it, probably completely puzzled still that his ceramic judgement had been so far out. He might even be wondering whether he ought to take the piece to the higher court of Sotheby's in London for a reversed verdict. I had no intention of allowing him to do that.

Edna had put on one bar of the electric heater, presumably thinking that was all I could afford, or my guest rated, and I didn't have to cough to make Geoffrey swing around. He crossed the room, took both my hands somewhat awkwardly, and went on for too long about how I shouldn't have got up for his sake when he was sure I wasn't fit enough as yet to manage the stairs. I asked him to switch on the other bar because I was still finding it a bit troublesome to bend over. We then settled in chairs facing each other with the red glow between us. It didn't take long to establish that this was the only glow between us.

Geoffrey had trained himself professionally never to allow the awkward silence to happen during interviews. As though half anticipating the threat of one of these, he started off at once on what a time it had been for all of us and how he had worried about what the newspapers would say, surprised that there had been so little lasting interest in the smashing of a heroin ring in the Highlands.

'You must be feeling relieved, Sophia, that the press has been so restrained about your part in all this?'

'That was my lawyer. He made it quite plain that they

had better be, and if they weren't they could find themselves up against a libel settlement that would cost them a lot more than any scandal about a woman of my years was worth. If I had been blonde and twenty-three and there had been the remotest possibility that I was Colin Gain's discarded mistress it might have been a different matter.'

'I see,' Geoffrey said, rather primly, I thought.

'Tea or coffee?' Edna asked from a door that we hadn't heard open.

Geoffrey said that he really didn't need anything at this time but was finally persuaded to have coffee. We then talked about his new home in Oban. He had been over to see it again, just a quick dash. The plaster was drying nicely and he could arrange for the fitting of the carpets any day now. It seemed best that he should be in Oban for the laying of these and so he had booked into an hotel there, cancelling his Loch Riddoch chalet. He was off in his little Metro in the morning.

I'm just not sure what I had come down expecting from Geoffrey; perhaps I was vain enough to believe it might be a proposal of marriage. This would have left me in the delightful position of having to refuse him, but gently, and possibly even to his relief, this leaving us both under the benediction of mutal kindness, the one towards the other. Instead he had come to tell me he was going to lay carpets in Oban.

He stayed for only ten minutes after tepid powdered coffee. Out on the drive he stood with one hand on the opened door of the Metro to make me promise to come and see him if I was ever in Oban. I said that I certainly would and hoped he would enjoy his cruises among the Hebridean islands.

I lingered on the front steps to watch him slide away. In that old dressing-gown I probably looked a bit like the witch latent in so many of us. I was certainly bringing my second sight to bear on Geoffrey's future. I saw him first in the carpeted Oban bungalow alone, but not for long. Three doors down, in another house of identical design, would be a lady whose husband had recently succumbed to a heart attack from too much gardening after a sedentary business life. The lonely ones would find that their interests were as interchangeable as their patio doors, and they would marry, but instead of bringing her widow's mite to swell Geoffrey's golden handshake she would hang on to what was hers, outlive him, so to collect his bounty money plus all Elspeth's careful hoardings from the Edinburgh years.

'What's he want then?' Edna asked from behind me.

'Nothing,' I said, turning to climb the stairs to go back to bed.

Dean sent us a cable from Mexico. It was addressed to me, but the love was for Aline. This troubled me somewhat. It would be personal disaster for the boy if distance started to make his heart grow fonder. If Aline was pleased to have the message to her she gave no sign, but then she sent out very few signs. Surprisingly, or at least to me, her training for summer work was going not too badly and she passed the test of our first batch of visitors with about a C-plus rating. These were two carloads from Leeds, eight in all, who wanted to sit together, so we joined up two tables and gave them three cakestands down the middle with the ketchup bottles in between. From the kitchen I would hear merry chaff about Aline as a bonny Highland lass, and once or twice the girl came back with a laden tray looking as though she just might have smiled.

Edna had left us, back to fishnet stockings, apparently content with what I had paid her for holding the fort at 'Morvern', but clearly disappointed that her good neighbour performance had really only resulted in anti-climax, with no startling revelations despite determined attempts to provoke these. If Pete missed Edna he had the grace, or the good sense, not to make a point of it. He needed someone to change him and his mother was careless about doing the job. Bayola seemed to be vindicating what the advertisements claimed for it, though I varied his diet with small, excruciatingly expensive tins of other food like spinach specially pulverized for infant stomachs. He was visibly growing, even to someone with him every day. After a nighmare in which I saw Pete suffocated under the eiderdown I went into Taybridge and bought a cot, mattress and small blankets, to which he took as though it was something he had been waiting for. Aline raised no objections to no longer having her son in bed with her.

Dean had arranged with a doctor in Taybridge to have Aline registered as an addict, with her heroin issued on prescription, and that I was to collect these, presumably of a decreasing dosage, at fortnightly intervals when I was in the town. I never saw what was in those boxes I brought back to 'Morvern', though I was told they contained daily ampoules for injection by Aline herself. The idea, I suppose, was that I issue the girl one of these every twenty-four hours, but when it came to doing that I simply could not. It wasn't that I didn't want the responsibility for doling out the drug, it was the feeling that it put me in a kind of authority which I couldn't assume and didn't feel right for our emerging relationship, if that was what was going to happen. Also, if a cure was possible at all, it wasn't going to be from someone else acting as policeman, it had to involve a postive effort of will on Aline's own part. The discipline must come from herself, it could not be imposed. And so I gave her the whole box, two weeks' supply, without ever opening it, and with no chat about Girl Guide's honour.

If she wanted to she could use two, three or more ampoules a day.

I never saw any sign that she had done this and I would have known all right. There was never any hint of serious withdrawal symptoms, of her being 'strung out' as Dean had called it. The only thing that did happen was that one night I was woken by my shoulder, which still troubled me if I got in certain positions, and after a time I thought I heard Pete crying. The sound went on and I got up and went along the twisting passage to the back bedroom.

It wasn't Pete who was crying, it was Aline. The sound of it dried out my mouth as I stood beyond a closed door, not loud, but from a desolation so deep and wide that I knew nothing I could say or do could possibly reach her. It was the weeping of a girl who finds herself in a whole world of strangers. I went back to bed.

CHAPTER 15

I have a theory that inflation is being organized with Machiavellian cunning by a whole posse of Big Brothers. For a time things are allowed to run on modestly enough, a penny or so on soap powder, two pennies on a tin of soup, with the next supermarket bay offering a much publicized reduction on dog food. This continues for weeks, even months sometimes, then it is the shock treatment, the order goes out that you are to be hit between the eyes by prices on every shelf, and no reductions anywhere. The shopping carriers still have to be filled, with customers coming out of the shops not really believing in what has been left behind from their purses at the checkout. They go home to bring out the last bottle of medium dry sherry for a quick one to help them face up to the future. The point of all this is that the shock treatment has worked, the bosses have got away with it; there have been no display windows broken, and the following week the increases are once again negligible, plus some reductions, and the customers are positively grateful that the manipulators have been so gentle.

I was thinking this coming home from Taybridge with a not very impressive heap of basic essentials sitting on the back seat for which I had paid out thirty-seven pounds, driving down a road which said that summer had come and which was overlooked by a green Ben Tala flatly denying that it had ever harboured deep snow. I was also thinking that I was going to have to work hard for the next four months when it would have been much nicer to be going off on holiday to Tenerife. By the time I had reached Loch Riddoch village I was wondering how much it was going to cost to have the motor-mower reconditioned, knowing that even if I got a bargain offer from someone for the job I couldn't afford to take it. Then, for some reason, as I turned into the gates of 'Morvern', I thought about Geoffrey in Oban walking over his new wall-to-wall floor coverings with never a twitch of worry about the rising cost of living.

There was a strange car parked by my door, a vintage mini-Morris, and it looked as though the vintage had gone off. The rear number plate was illegally covered in mud and it wouldn't have surprised me if the licence had been nine months out of date. Alongside that vehicle my Austin looked like a genteel symbol of middle-class security. I got out thinking about non-paying visitors, and with the feeling that whoever they might be they were unwelcome. I took my two carriers and went in. The front door was unlocked. I didn't really care for that now that the open season for door-to-door salesmen had started.

There were voices coming from the back sitting-room,

Aline's and another overlaying it, a woman's. I carried my
packages to the kitchen and put them on the table. There
were signs of tea having been made; Aline always left
signs of whatever she had been doing. I wondered where
Pete was. He would need changing. I went up the
backstairs to that bedroom. No baby. I came down again
and went into the little sitting-room without giving any
warning. It was, after all, my house.

On the whole 'Morvern' has in some way contrived to
remain immune to our boarders, almost as though it was
ignoring them. At times I've had the feeling it was
backing up my private comments on these visitors,
sustaining a joke between us. But from the moment I laid
eyes on the woman in the small sitting-room the joke
seemed to be on us, me and my house. I say 'woman'
though she couldn't have been much older than Aline,
but you can't be one of those who are instantly in control
of any environment or circumstance and go on being
classified as a girl. It wasn't her dress that had me slightly
unnerved, ballooning harem trousers with an
embroidered bolero jacket, we are quite used to this kind
of thing in the summer and last year there were rumours
of a topless caravaner doing her shopping in Menzies'
Self-Service; it was the lady's take-over bid. Her smile for
me was bright, from a largish mouth emphasized by
purple lipstick and big, very white teeth. Enormous hoop
earrings projected from under a bandana completely
covering hair which had to be dark if it matched eyebrows
needing plucking.

'You're Miss McLinn,' she told me, with no hesitation.

'I am. And who are you?'

'Tania!'

It was Aline who said that. I hadn't seen her really
nervous before, at least not in this way, on edge, so much
knocked out of her usual norm of indifference that there
were two spots of colour in her pale cheeks, these circular.

They might have been painted on for an appearance as a clown's assistant. Her voice was different, too, higher pitched.

'We used to share a flat in London. Tania has come all the way from Wales to see me.'

'*South* Wales,' Tania said, to make her performance in that battered relic outside all the more impressive. She added: 'I haven't seen Aline since she came north with that all-American boy. I told her she had flipped her brain to do it. Seems I was right.'

I am old-fashioned enough to be able to stiffen on occasion. I stiffened.

'My sympathies have been with the American boy,' I said.

Tania laughed.

'So I heard.'

'There's still some tea,' Aline announced, loud for her. 'I just made it a little while ago.'

'No, thank you. Where is Pete?'

'I put him out. In that carrycot you bought.'

'Out?'

'Just on the grass. It's sunny still.'

'There's a cold wind!'

I left the room, shutting the door, hearing the kind of laugh I would have expected from Tania. I went down towards the front door in a rage for which there was no logical explanation. Aline had put Pete in a corner against the outside wall of the house where the wind didn't get at him. He didn't need changing, which added to my resentment. He didn't even want to be picked up, and had been lying on his back with his legs in the air, fascinated by something in the sky, as though a golden eagle up there was staging a special show for the child's pleasure. Ben Tala was having one of its pushing closer to us days, looking much nearer than it was, and without a hint of the sinister, offering us valley dwellers its benediction.

I took deep breaths to help me return to some kind of composure but on a bright afternoon moving towards what was going to be a still bright evening this had no effect. It would be officious to pick Pete up and carry him inside, especially when he was enjoying himself. I left him and wandered across a lawn needing cutting, forcing on myself something I don't do very often, a little tour of the five-acre estate, with its sheds, and woods, and the last of the bluebells still putting colour into deep shade under the heavy evergreens.

I was in the shed where I kept my bicycle and the motor-mower, inspecting this for rust, when Aline found me.

'Miss McLinn . . . ?'

I turned. The shed has no window and she was blocking light from the door. I couldn't see her face clearly and she couldn't see mine.

'What is it?'

'Well, about Tania. The way she is with people she's just met. She doesn't mean to be like that. It's sort of . . . Oh hell!'

Quite a speech from Aline, which ought to be acknowledged.

'Your friends are none of my business,' I said.

'I can see you're angry still. At what she said about Dean.'

'Yes.'

'Well, it's sort of true, isn't it? For me, I mean? Isn't it?'

'How can I be expected to answer that?'

'No, you couldn't. Because it was only Dean you saw. You loved him.'

'Don't be ridiculous!'

'Oh God! I'm a fool! I'm always a fool when I try . . .'

She abandoned whatever she had been meaning to say.

I didn't attempt to help her, simply waited. The wait became rather absurd. Finally I had to say something.

'What is it you want, Aline?'

'What?' She had been in pursuit of her own thoughts for which there were no words. I heard her take a deep breath.

'Tania says . . . will you come to dinner with her tonight? At the hotel?'

'Is that where she's staying?'

'Oh no. She couldn't. I thought . . . if she was in my room you wouldn't mind. I mean, we won't need another bed or anything. And she's going in the morning. She has to get back.'

'I told you when you came, Aline, that what you did with your own room was your own business.'

'Oh. Then you will come to dinner?'

'What about Pete?'

'We'd leave him in the car. In the carrycot.'

'No. I'll babysit. You go.'

'You don't mind? I'd like to. A couple of drinks. It's . . . bloody dull here!'

'No need to shout at me!'

But she did it again, from the grass outside, turning her head:

'Bloody stupid dull!'

Then she began to run towards the house.

I don't really know why I did it, but after listening to the ten o'clock news that night I went up the back stairs to where Pete was asleep in his cot, lifting him out of this so carefully that I thought I had laid him on the big bed without his wakening until I saw his eyes open, watching me. I left him where he was, carrying the empty cot along to my own room, placing it at the foot of my bed. Pete made no sound when I went back for him, or when I was tucking him in under those small-sized blankets. Then I did something for which I can't really see a reason even now, I sat on the foot of my bed, on the folded quilt, pressing my hands together and with my knees holding them like a vice. There were tears in my eyes, but I didn't actually give way to them, and after a while I got up and went to the bathroom to wash my face. When I came back Pete seemed to be asleep, at least his eyes were shut.

Tania and Aline made a noisy return well after midnight. Even if I hadn't been lying looking at the dark ceiling the Mini would have wakened me, it had the kind of engine which coughs after it is switched off. Then doors banged, followed by crunching on the gravel which is all around my house like a first line of defence against intruders. The two of them breached a second line through the front door and Tania laughed when she must have been near the cigar store Indian. That was followed by another laugh that could only have been from Aline, something I had never heard before, not even when she was having a 'rush' after injecting herself. Not much of a laugh, on the thin side, but still a seal of approval on her evening, and a comment on all those other evenings here in 'Morvern' when she had simply endured because there was no possible alternative.

They must have gone up by the back stairs. I didn't hear them again after the kitchen door had shut, or Tania's voice sounding out like brass. Perhaps they made tea, or they may have brought a bottle back with them, taking it up to the bedroom. I lay waiting for Aline to come hunting for Pete, but she never did, needing him even less than usual that night.

I woke just after six with that bright light already across my bed which, in a late Scottish spring, tells us just how near we are to the Arctic. By the time I had dressed, changed and dressed Pete, it was getting on for seven, but it was still a total surprise to find Aline sitting at the kitchen table. She had made tea but seemed to have forgotten about it, a full cup between elbows propped on my scrubbed boards. Without taking her hands away from her jaws she looked up at Pete and me. I could see that drink and her prescribed drug weren't a good mix.

'Been keeping him from infection, have you?' she said.

Perhaps I deserved that. I certainly didn't offer any excuse for what I had done. There was something almost mechanical about the girl's dislike of me, as though more automatic than really personal. I was a symbol of her imprisonment in something from which she could see no escape. The personal had, at moments, showed signs of becoming a human relationship, certainly with a veering away from this before it was anything like established, but still the possibility there. Now, standing holding Aline's baby, I knew that the possibility no longer existed, that what she was beaming towards me would soon be hate, if it wasn't already.

I put Pete into the only chair with arms to hold him in, then went to the table to feel the teapot. It was cold. There were at least eight stubs in the ashtray. I was filling a kettle and had my back to her when she said, very loud, clearly turning in her chair to do it.

'How much money did Dean leave you for me?'

I put the lid on the kettle and took it to the stove, lighting the calor gas.

'He said it wasn't for you.'

'My board then? When I'm *earning* that. And a helluva lot more, too. A decent wage!'

'You may think so.'

'I asked how *much*?'

'Five hundred pounds.'

'My God!'

I was getting a cup and saucer when she asked: 'What have you done? Invested it in index-linked bonds?'

'It's in the bank.'

I took cup, saucer and plate over to the table, then put

out butter and marmalade and lit the grill to make toast.

'I want that money,' Aline said.

I took sliced bread from its preserving Cellophane.

She shouted: 'Don't you think I've earned it? Lying under Dean as his whore? For nearly a year?'

I had never been frightened of this girl, even of what she might do to herself, or Pete, during one of those withdrawal phases which she had tried to cover by staying in her room, so that I had only seen the fringes, hearing more than I saw. But as I stood near the grill watching toast I was close to fear from that new note in her voice, shrill, harsh, laden with some intent that had suddenly firmed in her mind.

'I'm leaving here!'

That was another shout. I took the toast out of the grill, put it in a rack, and brought it to the table. I then made fresh tea and sat down.

'Where are you going?' I asked.

'To a commune. In Wales. Where Tania is.'

'Is that the place for a drug cure?'

'To hell with a cure! To *hell* with it!'

'What about Pete?'

'I *knew* you'd ask that!'

'Well, I have, Aline. What about him?'

'He'll come too. There are kids there. Tania's Julie is there. What about Dean's money?'

'If you leave I'll send it back to him.'

'You damned old bitch! I could . . . !'

Her arm came out. She swept her cup and mine and the teapot on to the floor. I expected the noise to start Pete crying but it didn't. He was watching us, not moving. Aline stared down at shattered china, at the brown earthenware pot on its side. She began to sob. She put up her hands to her cheeks as though trying to hold her face into its proper shape. She was quite noisy. I sat thinking about what I had to do, the threat of fear gone, but not replaced by pity.

When the crying eased I said: 'If you take Pete with you to a commune, Aline, I'll alert the social services that you are a drug addict. And liable to bouts of uncontrollable violence. Totally unfit to look after a child.'

The sobbing stopped but her fingers still pushed at her cheeks.

I didn't hear the door to the back passage open. Tania shouted: 'What's going on in here? It sounded like a fucking riot!'

She was wearing, minus the tasselled cap that usually goes with it, one of those striped men's nightshirts advertised in the Sunday papers as a bedtime joke. It was outsize and the hem reached almost to her bare feet. Without that purple on her mouth she should have looked younger, but didn't. She came towards the table.

'Who started this?'

Neither of us answered. Aline took her hands away from her face and let them fall in her lap.

'You were both making enough noise a few minutes ago,' Tania said.

I looked up. 'I've just told Aline what I'll do if she tries to take Pete to your commune.'

The heavy eyebrows rose. 'Oh? I wouldn't have thought it was any of your business. I'll make some more tea.'

She bent for the pot, inspected it for cracks, found the lid and went to the sink. I went for a pan and brush and swept up the shattered china, clattering it all into a bin. Then I tackled the range, and by the time I had finished servicing it tea was ready, poured out in mugs. I sat down again but Tania stood close in to the table sipping, giving out a strong smell of sweat and flannel. She was staring at me.

'Look, Miss McLinn, I can gues what commune means to you. We all run round painted in woad except in winter when we wear goatskins. And the men horns. Okay?'

'I have never thought about communes,' I said, not managing to avoid sounding pompous.

'It's a farmhouse and chalets. They've got electric light and running hot and cold water. Not bad for kids. My Julie's doing fine. We work. I milk cows. We've got four. Goats, too. All that was done with money. You get in with a deposit. You don't if you haven't got it.'

'The deposit would be something like five hundred?' I suggested.

'Not nearly enough. Fifteen hundred rock bottom these days. Before I came up here I was hearing that we have room for about five still. No more. So entry money is Aline's little problem. Did Dean leave her five hundred?'

'No. He left it to me.'

Aline's head came up. 'She's keeping Dean's money!'

'No use, love, even if she didn't,' Tania said. 'I can't raise any. The Mini'd fetch about a hundred. With luck. Anyway, we need it down there. I'm on deliveries.'

Tania smiled at me.

'Vegetables. To the local town. Busy all the time, that's us. Like Disney's dwarfs. More like angels, we're that pure. If there was sin among us we couldn't have such clear eyes. Mine used to be bloodshot. Look at them now.'

I didn't look at them.

'There's something else,' she said. 'I stopped hitting it up. Heroin. Like this one here. I kicked the whole thing. Started before I went in the commune and finished after. And I mean finished. Look at these hands.'

She held them out over the table, strong fingers, nails not too clean, not a hint of a tremble.

'See? She'd have to work, too. If we could get her in. Kick the habit, maybe. Slow and easy. That's what I was telling her last night.'

Tania was strong enough to kick it, but Aline wouldn't

be. A voice, loud in my brain, was saying that. It could have been what I wanted to hear. Tania picked up her mug and made sucking noises as she drank. I stood up suddenly and went across the kitchen. At the door I nearly turned to ask one of them to look after Pete, only just checking that. I went along the hall and was four steps up the front stairs when it was as though my breath had been stolen from me, a weird sensation, I couldn't seem to make my lungs work. I had to grip the railing, first with one hand, then two. I hung on. Whatever this was it must not be allowed to happen. I made that a demand and it worked, breath was returned, as though the thief had repented. I didn't go slowly up the rest of the stairs. I wouldn't allow myself to do that.

My mother had what she called her 'strong box', but during the big clean-up after her death this went out and I now keep personal papers at the bottom of a sweater drawer. I took a bundle held together by elastic and went to sit on the unmade bed, momentarily distracted by my will, a large-sized document being impressive about what I am to leave behind. If the idea that was now in my mind developed the will's contents would have to be changed dramatically, the major beneficiary no longer being Oxfam. When he had drawn up the will for me some seven years earlier Mackenzie had been decidedly unhappy about the emphasis on Oxfam, suggesting that charity is all very well in its place but blood relations really ought to be given priority. I had said that I had never given my Edinburgh cousins any kind of priority while here and didn't propose they receive this after I'd left.

Beneath the will lurked two modest little books, one saying that I had seven hundred and forty-three pounds in a building society, the other giving me just over four hundred in Post Office Savings. If I used Dean's five hundred as well I would have enough to buy Aline into a commune in Wales.

CHAPTER 16

At first I felt guilt for what I had done, a nagging unease that was with me for much of the day. Then it was with me for much less of the day, the recurrences becoming infrequent enough to let me get rid of a fading shame by doing something active, like cleaning out a cupboard. Occasionally I'd look in a mirror wondering why wickedness didn't seem to be aging me. I certainly felt more cheerful than I had for a good many years. In Taybridge I found that I had three times the number of acquaintances than had been mine only weeks earlier, most of these people going out of their way to comment on my glowing appearance, as though they now thought there must be something tonic about being shot, provided you didn't get the bullet in the wrong place.

The citizens of Loch Riddoch village were much more reserved. At first they had seemed to enjoy the publicity the Gain affair had brought but were now having acute second thoughts. For one thing, curiosity brought the wrong kind of tourists, short-stay trippers who came to stare but not spend money. Also, most unfairly, I was held to be at least semi-responsible for one of our local boys waiting trial on a drug charge, which meant the garage had closed down, a great inconvenience. We were into the season of door-to-door charity collections but the rose-growing ladies in headscarves didn't bring their Lifeboat Institution or Red Cross books to 'Morvern' even though in recent years I had upped my contribution to these worthy causes from fifty pence to seventy-five. I was told that the local minister had preached a sermon in which, though I didn't actually receive dishonourable mention, he referred to dark forces at work in our community, and it was pretty obvious that the clack over teacups sometimes included sinister suggestions that Colin Gain must have had a better reason for wanting me dead than the one I had put forward, and which the police had been willing to accept.

The long-absent Maureen came back after Edna and Aline had gone, but she wasn't her old gossipy self at all, and I got the feeling that if she hadn't needed the money 'Morvern' would not have seen her. With paying guests in the house, and me mostly in the kitchen, we didn't meet much except for coffee, and these were far from cosy sessions, Maureen polite, but her mouth practically buttoned up, the weather our basic topic. Also, unlike Edna, she was highly reserved with Pete, as though by practically ignoring him she kept at bay any risk of becoming emotionally involved with the new life patterns in my home.

With all the hard work involved in keeping up to twelve people reasonably content, as well as organizing a baby's day, my conscience practically closed down, though there was one scene connected with Aline that did recur, sometimes when I was least expecting it. I would see again the two about to leave, with Tania standing to look at me across the low roof of the Mini, Aline already inside. Pete was out of sight, in his carrycot, at the sheltered side of the house. I had waited in real tension for Aline to go around to see him, certain that she would, if only for my benefit, but she didn't, just went straight to the car, dressed for the journey as she had been to come to me in the night, her load the same, too, except for a baby. She didn't say goodbye, or even look at me. It was Tania who stared.

It was that stare which remained much more of a threat to my peace than anything I had done to Aline. From it I knew that if Tania ever had a chance to strike at me she would take it, and the frightening thought was that she might try to do this through Pete.

I didn't go to see my lawyer in Taybridge until I was summoned by him, and I knew what had brought that about, he had just heard that Pete was now in what looked like permanent residence. I found Mackenzie sufficiently rallied from the distresses of his professional connection with Colin Gain to be able to concentrate entirely on me, and with at least eighty per cent of his old authoritarian manner. In the first fifteen minutes he contrived to put over the thought that it might be his painful duty in the not too distant future to have me committed to a mental institution. He pointed out, what I already knew, that the arrangements I had made for looking after Pete were legally indefensible, nothing more than an unofficial fostering which the child's mother could challenge at any time, even if she had given me some form of declaration in writing. When I said that I had no such declaration from Aline he made what I can only describe as a clucking noise, and when I went on to state that the fact Aline could have the boy back at any time was something I could live with, he just shook his head.

He made a break about then to send for coffee and only when I was properly fortified by a weak solution did he broach the delicate matter of my being far too old to raise a child, particularly a male child. I said that I did realize there would be problems, but none that we couldn't meet together if he would agree to function as a kind of informal godfather. At this the poor man, believing I was serious, was for a moment almost unable to disguise panic. In the end, however, having completely covered himself against the remotest possibility of becoming personally, rather than professionally, involved in any mess I might create, we parted amicably enough, almost with his good wishes that I would survive successfully all the ordeals which certainly lay ahead.

I suppose my living is a kind of gamble, but every day which passes with no phone call from Wales, no letter, and especially no aged Mini coming up the drive, puts just a fraction more weight on the odds in my favour. I would never have subjected myself to the stress of all this if I hadn't been pretty certain that once Aline had lived away from Pete for any length of time she wouldn't want the inconvenience of having him back. I could be very much underestimating the power of maternal feelings, though in this case I don't think I am.

But I have no right to attempt an assessment of Aline's feelings, I never really tried to get to know her. And that made it much easier for me when it came to buying her baby, using Dean's money and my own. When I had done it I wrote to tell Dean that his girl had gone off with Tania to grow vegetables in Wales and, probably, to commune with the Infinite under the long-distance guidance of a Hindu guru operating from a cave in the Himalayas. The point I tried to make very plain was that he was now free to get on with his own life in Mexico. It took him more than two months to react to that with a postcard from Puerto La Cruz in Venezuela, eleven words in the message, not one of them even hinting at continuing pain in the region of his heart.

About the middle of September the last tour bus comes through Loch Riddoch en route to wherever those things hibernate in winter, a signal that we are moving into the season when picnic sites will no longer be sprayed with litter and the locals can use their cars with a diminishing risk of killing foreigners, particularly the French, who tend to drive on the right side of the road for them, but the wrong for us.

I had two lots of visitors during the month, one early, one late, but in between a gap in which I could relax, at least in the afternoons after Maureen had gone home. We had three days of continuous sunshine, a season's record, the last of these really hot, seeing me out on the grass in a deckchair with Pete on a rug. He needed watching these days, having evolved a game of waiting until I seemed to be asleep before taking off on extensive explorations of new territory. I would open my eyes to find him a good ten yards away, travelling at some speed, this broken by pauses to put something in his mouth. It was a phase I was hoping wouldn't last long because these objects, often stones, weren't easy to get out of his mouth. At first I had been terrified he would swallow and then choke before I could do anything, but I soon learned that if you turn them upside down quickly, and hold them that way during the extraction, the worst doesn't happen. When I write my book on baby care for aging spinsters I'm putting in a section on stone swallowing; none of the standard guides I've seen mention it.

I woke from a doze to the sound of tyres crunching on gravel. Our postal service has been rationalized to one delivery a day in the afternoon, that is except when Fat Tam decides that what looks like another bill for Miss McLinn can just as well wait until tomorrow. Tam never hurries, either in his red van or on his feet, but when, after minutes, there was no repeat sound of tyres going away, I turned to look towards the front drive.

The man who must have been ringing the doorbell to no effect was now coming across the grass towards me. He looked a tourist of the better sort, not one of the kind hand picked by Willie Menzies to send to me, what my mother would have called a 'gent'. He seemed just slightly unhappy in a holiday outfit of blue turtle-necked sweater and trousers to tone, giving the feeling they might have been chosen for him by his wife. I got out of my deckchair with the usual struggle and was all ready with my piece about not taking bed and breakfast casuals when the man stopped and said:

'You won't remember me, Miss McLinn?'

It took me some moments to identify the Inspector Wilcott with whom I had, months before, exchanged smiles in my kitchen and perhaps a dozen words in my front hall. That he should be visiting me now was a considerable surprise and apparently the call was social, starting with his explanation that he was on holiday with his wife and that they were stopping for two nights at the Loch Riddoch Hotel. Then, standing with his back to my somewhat grim stone house, he paid Ben Tala and the view a compliment. There was only one deckchair so we moved to a bench on the gravel patch from which I could still keep an eye on Pete, who was now sitting up thinking about how he might entertain himself.

The inspector's trousers were a shade too tight for a mature figure, something of which he was conscious, and I made a point of not watching while he fought to get his tobacco pouch out of one pocket and pipe from the other.

'We've had five days at the Edinburgh Festival,' he announced suddenly.

It had been his wife's idea, something she had wanted to do for a very long time, an experience that may have been rewarding for her, but didn't seem to have done much for the inspector. I asked what they had seen and heard and he gave me a dogged inventory of crowded days and nights, everything in proper sequence. As a reward for his having been docile about intensive culture, his wife had allowed him to take her into the wilds of the Highlands, though her first reaction to the beauties of our valley had been a headache that had made her skip lunch and take to bed for the afternoon.

It wasn't long before the inspector and I got on to the only topic which we really had in common: Colin Gain. He told me that no man had ever had better natural cover for his role as a Mr Big in the heroin trade. It was almost as though the cover had been waiting for him to be born into it.

'Building the right cover is the hardest part of a villain's business, Miss McLinn. That is, if he plans to go at one thing steadily over the years with any hope of getting away with it. Gain had all that as a gift. And part of the gift was the fact that everyone around here expected a certain flamboyance from their young laird. Natural after the mother he had, apparently. That's what I got out of talking to people in the village. It was almost as though they approved of the villa in Greece and the stories of his women.'

'It certainly gave us an interest,' I said. 'Inspector, you were obviously brought to this district by pointers to it as the base for a heroin operation. Didn't Colin's flamboyant lifestyle interest you?'

He was watching Pete, who now seemed to be considering a crawl dash.

'On a job like this *everyone's* lifestyle interests a policeman. There was a check on Gain. But what did we turn up? Almost the playboy by inheritance. His father lost a lot of money on horses. The family's English estates went that way. But the son seemed to be doing all right with his house turned into the rich man's alternative to joining a shooting syndicate. Gain was obviously making money, some of it from roulette on the side. But I wasn't looking for anyone running gambling without a licence. Not my job. As drug squad, I was only a guest in Scotland. Your local police are touchy. Almost as bad up here as in Italy. And that's a place I don't like working in.'

The inspector got about the world. I had the thought then that he wasn't the kind of man likely to return to the scene of a case that was closed, even to savour a success. And I could think of better places than the Loch Riddoch Hotel in which to recover from a Festival of Music and Drama.

'He lost his nerve, Miss McLinn. Surprising in a man like that. Yet I think I can see why. He'd kept his organization up here tight over the years, using the minimum of people. The possibility that you'd identified him as being in Loch Riddoch when he should have been in Rhodes was probably the first threat to his security in this place. He came after you because he had to find out who you were. And the identification really worried him. It would have worried me in his shoes.'

'Am I to take that as a compliment, Inspector?'

'If you like.'

'I couldn't have been the first threat to his security. He killed to get rid of that.'

Wilcott's head jerked around to me.

'*What*? Oh, I see. You mean his number two, Menzies? Gain didn't shoot him.'

It was a moment before I said: 'Our police believe he did.'

'Believe isn't the word I would have used. They want a tidy file. It's a temptation I have to live with, too. We are all subject to statistics. Hanging over us is that threat of percentage failures against percentage successes. Give me one good reason why Gain would want to shoot his right-hand man?'

'A quarrel. About profits.'

'Was that in the official handout to the press? For my money, Miss McLinn, it makes a sick motive. I'm speaking as a guest in Scotland, of course. But also as something of a specialist in my own field. There is a lot of killing in the heroin business. It's a high risk enterprise in terms of that as well as being caught. But you only kill for betrayal. And no one has turned up even a hint of a suggestion that Menzies ever contemplated any kind of sellout of his boss. If there was anything else heavily on Gain's mind at the time he thought you'd identified him, it would have been that he hadn't been able to contact

Menzies on this visit to Loch Riddoch. It was worrying him enough for him to get in touch with the garage man about it. Usually there was no direct contact between them.'

Pete had suddenly gone into action, moving at speed across the grass. I went to retrieve him. Wilcott was standing at the edge of the rug when I got back with my captive.

'I wouldn't have thought of you as a babysitter,' he said. 'Some relation's child?'

'No. Aline's boy. You remember her?'

'Of course I do. Is she still with you?'

'No. Gone south.'

'On a cure?'

'Of a sort.'

'I see. That must leave you with your hands full. Is this arrangement likely to go on for some time?'

'Perhaps indefinitely.'

He kept astonishment nicely under control.

'Isn't that quite some responsibility?'

'You should have added "at my age", Inspector. Thank you for not doing it.'

'This has nothing to do with me,' he said.

But I got the impression that it *did* have something to do with him, and that he was disturbed. I said I would make tea if he would look after Pete, leaving them together, glancing back from a corner of the house to see him already down on his knees on the rug, a hint of father training at some period. I then had the totally irrelevant thought that when my final batch of guests had gone I would get in touch with McFie about the bitch he had offered. Two females in the house would be a counter to a growing male influence. I had the ridiculous feeling that Ming would have minded a dog as his replacement, but would have given his approval to the idea of a bitch.

As I crossed the grass carrying a tray Wilcott gave up

the game he had been playing with a wooden engine, Pete watching this with moderate interest. The inspector might have been a child pyschologist applying a test first evolved by the Jungian school. He was able to give me a favourable verdict.

'He's going to be very bright, Miss McLinn.'

'If you can tell at that age it's more than I can. Some days I think yes, some days no.'

Wilcott got to his feet, then asked, 'Don't you find all this keeps you very tied?'

'Yes. But then I'm tied anyway. By lack of money.'

'Aren't you being paid for what you're doing?'

'By Aline? Hardly.'

'So it's a charity?'

'I hadn't thought of it as that. But I might. Would you suggest a contribution box on the hall table?'

He didn't laugh. He took the tray and we went to the bench with it. When we were settled he looked at me and I believe was considering saying that not many women in my position would do what I was doing, but he thought better of it and helped himself to a digestive biscuit. I poured tea. I would have had him weight-watching on no milk or sugar, but he took both. I went over to the rug with a small portion of biscuit just to give Pete the feel of something in his mouth. There was a question I wanted to put to the inspector, but I was having difficulty in shaping it. Beside him again I forced it out.

'When you were up here on the case did you follow up any other leads on who killed Murdo? I mean, since you're so sure it wasn't Colin?'

'No. For one thing I wasn't sure then. For another it wasn't my place to challenge what were becoming the conclusions of your local force. As I told you, establishing Gain as the killer kept everything tidy. Further developments could have become very messy indeed.'

'Then what made you go on thinking about the case

after the file had been closed?'

'An interesting question, Miss McLinn. Do you do crosswords?'

'No, I hate them.'

'Could that be because you want to use words, not play with them?'

'I've no idea.' I thought about Geoffrey then, who had so obviously failed to respect my confidence when under gentle interrogation from the police.

'I'm an addict,' Wilcott said. 'So much so that I have to ration myself to two a week. And when I can't manage to get one of the clues I can be haunted for days by those empty squares. My wife gets somewhat irritated when I wake up with the answer in the middle of the night and have to go padding downstairs to fish out a newspaper I've kept in a drawer for a week. It's a form of insanity.'

'But which has its uses? Was it in the middle of the night that you suddenly came up with the name of Murdo's killer?'

'No. It was on a plane between Bonn and Zürich.'

'Now that you know, what are you going to do about it?'

'Nothing. The evidence is so thin in terms of a prosecution that a defence lawyer would have it in shreds in no time. Totally circumstantial except on one or two points, and these are shaky. But even if it had been possible to build up a strong case I just might have found myself torn between a policeman's duty and personal inclination.'

'I take it you mean *not* to name the killer?'

'That's right.'

'Inspector, did you come here today specially to tell me all this?'

'Yes.'

'Why?'

'Increasingly I felt it was important that you know

about the conclusion I reached on that plane. I believe
you shot Murdo Menzies.'

After a moment I laughed. It wasn't a bad reaction to
being suddenly accused of murder, a bit short and
sharpish, perhaps, but still a laugh. I then emptied out
half a cup of cold tea on the gravel and poured myself
another from the pot. I wasn't aware of Wilcott watching
for my reactions, but he may have been. I was conscious
of the tea as sustaining. It put an element of the ordinary
into a very abnormal situation. When I looked at the man
beside me it was to see him looking at the mountain. Ben
Tala was still cloud free and sunlit. One of my secret
follies is to believe in omens, and the mountain's moods
are included in these. I felt calm enough to put the
question I was pretty sure he was waiting to answer.

'What are the non-circumstantial bits of evidence,
Inspector?'

He smiled. It might almost have been to encourage me.
I was reminded of the way he had smiled across my
kitchen months before. His tone was conversational.

'On the day it has been established that Menzies died,
Miss McLinn, you were at the McFie farm in the early
afternoon. The road to the farm takes you past the spot
where the killing took place. Do you remember going to
see the McFies on that day?'

'I remember going up to the farm on *a* day about that
time. But hasn't it been impossible forensically to
establish the exact day on which Murdo died?'

'A point for the defence,' he said, without turning his
head from watching Pete. 'However, there is contributory
evidence which makes it highly probable that the day of
your excursion was the day of the killing. So shall we
accept that as established fact for the moment?'

'If you insist.'

He gave me a quick look. I had been ready for it.
Something in my manner seemed to irritate him. His

voice hardened.

'Jock, the garage man, had a rendezvous with Menzies on the afternoon of the day in question. This was to be where the killing took place. Apparently Menzies always made a point of playing the fisherman at these rendezvous. And playing isn't the right word. He was keen on the sport. He really fished. That isn't something you can hurry. Which meant that he was usually on the scene for a considerable time before, or after, these appointments he had with Jock, usually at that particular spot. Incidentally, do you remember why you went up to the McFies' farm that day?'

'Of course. To see about the broilers I get from them in summer. I'd heard that Marian McFie was cutting down on her hens and I wanted to know whether that would affect deliveries to me. I'd forgotten that she and her husband were in Canada visiting their son. But Jessie, who helps them, was there feeding the hens. She must have told you about my visit.'

He had no comment on that. It was a moment before he asked.

'On your way home did you see Menzies out on that promontory fishing?'

'I may have seen someone out there, but I can't remember.'

'I see. You choose not to answer that one. Well, perhaps you will answer this? Can you explain why you were seen *again* on that road which passes the murder site, *again* coming along it towards Loch Riddoch village, this roughly only within an hour or so of the time you had used that road coming from the farm? But on this occasion you weren't in your car, you were riding a *bicycle?*'

'What am I being asked to explain, Inspector? Why I used the road twice that afternoon, or why I used my bicycle?'

'Both!'

'Very well. I used my bicycle the second time to save petrol. I couldn't go to the McFie farm on it, it's too far and a very steep push up at the end. So I used the Austin for that trip. I was home and had put the car away when I remembered I was almost out of pine cones. There had been a strong wind the night before which meant a lot would have blown down. I use them as firelighters. I soak them in paraffin and they're a lot more effective and very much cheaper than the bought things. But not if you use petrol to collect them. So, as I always do for these excursions, I got out my bicycle. Who was it that saw me on it? I didn't see anyone.'

'That could be, Miss McLinn, because you were going too fast at the time to spot our witness. He was parked in his van up one of those forestry tracks.'

'Who was it saw me?'

'The garage man. Menzies was a stickler about the timing of these appointments for the exchange of heroin. They were over in minutes.'

'And Jock had arrived too soon?'

'Yes. He'd been out repairing a tractor. There was no point in going home.'

'I see. So half hidden up that track smoking a cigarette he looked up from his girlie magazine to see me go whizzing past.'

'That's more or less it.'

'He's prepared to swear it was me on the bicycle.'

'No, he isn't. He just thinks it was you.'

'I take it the local police have failed to see any likely connection between me out collecting pine cones and a murder a mile or two up the road *possibly* on the same day.'

'You're right there. You know, Miss McLinn, I can't help wondering what you would have done if you had spotted the garage man. After all, you'd been pretty careful about no one seeing you up to that point.'

'I don't follow?'

'Well, having seen from your car Menzies out on that point you came back on your bicycle because on that machine, and on a fairly lonely road, you would have heard any traffic coming in time to hide both yourself and your transport. The garage man would have been a threat. Liable to blow your carefully arranged cover.'

I looked straight at Wilcott then.

'There's only one thing I could have done, Inspector. I'd have got off my bike, leaned it against a tree, then walked over to shoot Jock. Now tell me that the murder weapon has been found.'

'No, it hasn't.'

'Not even a hint as to where I kept a gun in my house from one of my numerous summer staff? All of whom have been through my drawers.'

'Not a hint.'

'What makes you think I had a gun?'

'It could be your Service record. Quite a few came back to civilian life with little mementoes like a .45.'

'All right, you've equipped me with a gun. But you haven't given me a motive. I have never pretended to like Murdo and a good two-thirds of the village are with me there. But we'd have a highly murderous local society if dislike meant you went out and killed.'

'And yet, Miss McLinn, isn't that what Murdo Menzies did?'

'What on earth do you mean?'

'He disliked you. So he killed your dog.'

I stared at the man.

'Are you saying that I shot Murdo as a revenge killing for what he did to my Chow?'

'Not exactly.'

'*Not exactly*? This is lunacy!'

Wilcott's voice stayed quiet.

'I rather expected that you would try to get me on the run,' he said. 'But you're not going to. So we'll just slow down, shall we? Look at things without getting heated. But first you'd better look after the boy. He seems to be eating something out there on the grass.'

The interruption took the better part of ten minutes. I had to catch Pete, get the stone out, set him back on the rug, then go to the front hall for his carrycot which has sides firm enough to hold him in, at least for a time. When I got back to the bench the Inspector had his pipe going again. I sat down, the tea tray a barrier between us.

'Ready?' he asked politely.

'Yes.'

'To get back to the dog. He wasn't just shot.'

'I don't want to hear about it!'

'But you're going to. McFie found him, didn't he? Just as he found Gain. A dog who never strayed far from home found nine miles from this house, up a glen, on a steep slope. He knew the animal. He rang you. You came out. He expected you to be in a very distressed state. But what he remembers now is how calm you were.'

'What is the point of all this?'

'The point is, Miss McLinn, how much what happened mattered to you. Your dog wasn't just shot. He had been maimed first. After having been lured into a car or a van and taken to that hillside. One of his back legs was almost severed. McFie had never seen anything like it. There was a blood trail for two hundred yards. With the poor beast dragging itself down the hill, to where the killer had gone to wait. It was probably a long time before that final bullet into the dog's skull . . .'

'For God's sake stop this!'

'You hated him, Miss McLinn. You hated Murdo Menzies.'

'Yes! I hated him!'

'You asked for a motive!' Wilcott said, then added: 'I'm sorry.'

I think he had expected me to cry. I didn't. I didn't look at him, but I didn't cry. His voice went on, in a flat tone, almost as though he was dictating to a machine.

'You asked McFie to bury your Chow. You said something to him about tinkers in the district and Glasgow skinheads at the caravan site. You didn't want anything said in the village about the killing. You told him you would report the matter to the police in Taybridge. Did you?'

'Yes. By telephone.'

'There's no record of it.'

'That's not my fault,' I said.

'Nor theirs. Because you didn't do it. You didn't phone in that report because you knew if you did the news would get back to the village via the local constable. To be the talk in the pub. And the last thing you wanted was to have the people here saying that once again Murdo Menzies had demonstrated that he could do anything he liked and get away with it. Because he was a Menzies. Heir to the ruling family in Loch Riddoch village. Isn't that right?'

I didn't say anything.

'You decided on no apparent reaction at all,' Wilcott told me. 'You decided to wait for the day when you could confront the man, with terror your weapon. You wanted to make him confess to what he had done to your dog. To really frighten someone like Menzies there had to be a gun in your hand.'

Pete was climbing over the side of the carrycot. I watched that for a moment before reacting to the Inspector's assessment of my plans. Then I said: 'In doing your crosswords have you ever brooded over a clue, and then were certain you'd found what you needed, because it fitted and seemed to look all right? But the next day the printed solution showed you were wrong?'

'It can happen,' he said.

'It happened this time. Murdo Menzies was not murdered by me.'

'I didn't use the word murder, Miss McLinn. I said you shot him.'

In surprise I looked at him. He was looking at me. I don't think I have ever seen an intelligent face offering so little expression. We might have been chatting about trivia that bored him.

'I go there with a gun,' I said. 'Having driven all the way home to get it, then come back on my bicycle to confront Murdo as you call it. As a result of this confrontation I shoot him. That's not murder?'

'In some circumstances it could be self-defence.'

'How?'

'It depends on your intent. I think it was your intention to have Menzies grovel in fear for his life. You weren't going to kill him. All you wanted was that confession. In other words, to win. To kill him wouldn't be winning. The vanquished must go on living for the victor's satisfaction.'

I didn't look at him with my next question.

'So what, as you see it, went wrong?'

'Menzies refused to grovel. I think he probably got up and came towards you, making that a flat challenge to use your gun before he disarmed you. And he didn't think you'd have the guts to pull that trigger. He was used to winning, always. Was sure he would then. You had seconds for your decision. To accept total defeat from that man. Or not. You remembered how to use that handgun. You'd had training in the firing of a .45. Live rounds on an Army range. You raised your arm, aimed, and pulled the trigger. The bullet opened his skull. But I imagine there was time for him to show surprise. And for you to see it.'

The Inspector permitted a silence. Though there were clouds in the sky, as there nearly always are in the Highlands, not one of them looked like coming near the summit of Ben Tala. The mountain seemed to shine with its own light.

'I think you had better have another look at your clues,' I said.

I stood up.

'There are wasps about. I'll get the tea things into the kitchen.'

I bent for the tray, then straightened holding it, looking down at him.

'Why did you say that you felt I *ought* to know you believed I had shot Murdo?'

'Some secrets are too oppressive to live with, Miss McLinn. At least for most of us. In time they have to be let out.'

'Is that from your experience as a policeman?'

'Yes.'

He started putting away the tobacco pouch, not easy in those trousers, a considerable squirming on the bench.

'Are you talking about conscience, Inspector?'

'You might call it that, I suppose. At least the need to share that secret with someone. I've seen it a good few times. When it hits it hits hard. The most perfect cover is no longer any use. You have to come out from behind it. You can't go on walking alone with the shadow. You have to tell someone.'

'Telling is the therapy?'

'That's about it.'

'Have I been getting the treatment before there are any signs that I need it?'

'Could be. Well, I must go, Miss McLinn. The wife will soon be wanting a drink. Best of luck with the boy.'

He got up, nodded, then walked towards the drive. I walked the other way with the tray, to the kitchen. When

I came out of the house there wasn't even the crunch of tyres on gravel, just the whine of an engine from somewhere near the humped bridge. I went over to the rug and squatted down beside Pete, suddenly realizing that he had done something he had never done before, climbed out of the carrycot and then climbed back in, a complete, rounded operation.

I was going to need time for this boy. Eighteen years at least. Twenty plus would be better, but I must have the eighteen. I meant to take them.